DAWN OF A THOUSAND SUNSETS

MORTALITY BITES SERIES

RAMY VANCE

KEEP EVOLVING STUDIOS

DAWN OF A THOUSAND SUNSETS

PART I
A BEGINNING OF SORTS

NEW YEAR'S DAY (six hours in)—

"Of course there's a samurai," I said as the beast of a man swung his giant naginata at me. I ducked under the bladed spear and briefly thought I could make a dash for the bridge behind, but I caught a glimpse of his left heel as he pivoted. His body twisted around like a fidget spinner before bringing the blade of his naginata in a low swoop.

I saw what he was trying to do. He wanted me to try to run past him so he could slice me in half with the blade. Cheeky little bastard.

The sword mounted on his spear swung harmlessly through the air, though "harmless" may have been an understatement. That blade was so sharp I was sure air molecules were being turned into air mulch. *Is that even scientifically possible?*

"First, huh? What do you mean 'scientifically possible?' " Keiko said. "And second, I already told you: he is the legendary Benkei. Benkei is *not* samurai." From the corner of my eye I watched as Keiko cut down a shisa guardian dog with her sword. The poor creature didn't stand a chance, falling into two pieces before her feet. "He is a warrior monk. There's a difference."

"You say 'potato,' I say, 'scary mythical dudes with half-moon spears po-*ta*-to,' " I said, deflecting his naginata with my dirk. "Now's not the time to split hairs."

Several gunshots rang out and I turned to see Jean empty his pistol into three more shisa clamoring down from caves in the cavern's walls. "I don't know," Jean said. "Profiling is terrible. I mean, would you like it if people referred to you as a baby in a kilt?" He managed to give me a smirk as he shot a fourth shisa without even looking in its direction. Show-off.

"Cherub *mask*!" I cried out as the warrior monk upgraded his naginata for a nokogiri, a Japanese double-edged saw with a two-foot-long hilt normally used by farmers to hew down trees. Either this guy thought I was made of wood, or he really enjoyed chopping at people with sharp thingies.

I managed to roll out of the way just in time for him to stick the cave floor with its blade. Hard. As in, stuck-in-stone hard. His nokogiri was stuck. Sure, given his strength and speed he'd pull it out in a second, but a second was all I needed.

I pivoted before jumping on his nokogiri, using the wooden shaft of his weapon as a balancing beam. I ran up it and kicked him in the face. I got him right in his samurai demon mask's nose and the blow knocked him back so hard he let go of his bladed spear.

Score one for Ms. Darling.

And as if my move wasn't epic enough, I leapt over him, putting myself between the monk and the bridge he was guarding. All I needed to do now was run along the rope bridge to the other side, where my soul was being held captive in some jar or bowl or Tupperware or whatever it was souls were stored in these days.

I had lost my soul a few weeks earlier when I had been temporarily turned back into a vampire. I had to admit, living without a soul had been … *empty*. To say I wanted it back was a dire understatement and it was only a few feet away. I could barely contain my fervor as I ran across the rope bridge.

But my celebrations were short-lived. The warrior monk went old school, pulling out a good ol'-fashioned sledgehammer. And I do mean a sledgehammer; there was no fancy Japanese name for it—just a hammer. A hammer by any other name and all that.

"Watch out for his hizuchi," Keiko said as if I hadn't seen the six-inch flat bit of the hammer swinging through the air. A "hizuchi"—so much for no fancy Japanese name.

I figured he was going to chase after me and nail me right through the wooden bridge's planks and down to the cave floor hundreds of feet below. Well, screw that. If anyone was going to end me Wile E. Coyote style, they'd have to do it to my face.

I stopped and turned to face him, placing a hand on the bridge's rope railing. He was heavy and the second he stepped onto the bridge the thing would start shaking. A lot. Possibly enough to knock me off and save him the trouble.

Maybe he was counting on that, too. Much more efficient than sledgehammering me.

But the monk didn't charge toward me. Instead he removed his demon mask, revealing a pleasant, youthful face. He narrowed his eyes and pursed his lips as if conflicted.

What could he possibly be conflicted about? I thought. He wanted to stop me from getting to the other side and the only way to do so would be to engage me here on the bridge. Right?

I barely had time to consider what else was running through the ancient warrior's mind when he swung his hizuchi like a golf club, knocking out the pegs that secured the ropes to his side of the bridge.

He'd figured out an even more efficient method of killing me.

The bridge dipped away and just like that, I was airborne. I didn't have a chance.

As I fell, I wondered what dying without a soul does to a person.

1
JAPAN AIRLINES ... THE SOUL OF THE SKY

 2 HOURS BEFORE THE NEW YEAR—

I always liked the soft hum of an airplane engine. It was a constant, soothing sound that permeated the cabin, a sound that—as long as it played its steady tune—meant all was right with the plane, and by extension, the world. And this plane hummed with all the reassurance of a mother's lullaby.

If I could only bottle the feeling that sound gave me, I thought.

"What feeling?" Deirdre asked.

I lifted a cautionary finger, not removing my sleeping mask from my face. "No listening in on my thoughts, Deirdre."

"But milady, you said that out loud," she said in a very serious tone. After all the time I'd spent with my changeling friend, she knew I had a habit of thinking out loud. But she always commented, even though she must have known the thought wasn't directed at her.

"Did I?" I said, hoping my intonation would reinforce the rhetorical nature of my question.

"You did."

So much for that. I removed the mask and looked at Deirdre, who sat upright in the booth next to me. I, on the other hand, was about seventeen degrees from lying flat, my body inclined, my feet hanging out on the cushion provided in the first-class Nippon Airways pod.

It was good to have money.

"You're too tense," I said, making eye contact with the stewardess who immediately came over with a glass of champagne. "Enjoy this. We do, after all, have about nine hours left on this flight."

Deirdre shook her head, her anxious face morphing into one racked with worry. "I cannot. Not with such an important mission before us. We must retrieve your soul and I swear by the GoneGods I will smite anyone who—"

So that was what she was so tense about. The mission. Our little jaunt to the other side of the world, where my soul was supposedly chilling in some jar.

A few days ago, I'd had no idea my soul had been ripped away from me. Not that there weren't clues. A crushing, never-ending pit of despair overshadowing my generally sunny disposition, for one. But also I was being stalked via two-way radio by this weirdo with a raspy voice who claimed that not only was my soul lost, so was his.

Raspy Man said we were soul-less mates. Hilarious. But after a while, even I had to admit he might have a point; the emptiness within me was undeniable. That, plus the little detail of having a magical amulet in my possession that had answered the question I wished most to know.

Where am I?" I had asked it, by which I had meant: Where is the part of me that makes me, *me*? Where is my soul?

It had told me that not only was my soul missing, but it had also drawn a map on my left forearm.

Like a tattoo. An ugly, morphing, magical tattoo.

I hated tattoos.

I groaned, cutting Deirdre off. She gave me a familiar look of confusion and hurt—the one that simultaneously said, *"I have disappointed you. My apologies,"* and *"I am only trying to help you, selfish bitch."*

And she was right. I mean, I'd only had to tell her what was going on and the changeling warrior had her bag packed before I'd even finished the story.

I took the changeling's hands in mine. "Deirdre, honey," I said in a patronizing tone worthy of my mother. "First of all, thank you so, so, so much for your concern, but there is absolutely nothing we can do about that on this plane. Look around. We're in first class. Enjoy the luxury now, smite the enemy later. I spent a fortune on these tickets, and—"

"I thought you said you got a deal because we were flying two days before New Year's."

"I did. But a deal in first class is still first class. The tickets still cost me my first born's college fund."

"I shall work to help replenish your dwindling finances."

"Deirdre," I said, trying to break through the fae's over-eagerness, "that was a joke. I have plenty of money. I was a forward-planning vampire with lots of assets and a diversified investment plan. I even have a 401k. And now that I'm human, I don't have to worry about living forever, so it's time to *enjoy* what I built up for the last three hundred years. So please, help me on that mission. The mission to enjoy."

She pursed her lips in answer.

"Please. Try—for me."

Deirdre paused for a long moment before nodding. "I shall try, but this metal dragon is so ... so unnatural and—"

"She's not worried about the mission," Egya cackled from a pod across the aisle. "She doesn't like flying."

The Ghanaian had been un-characteristically quiet this whole flight so far because, as he'd put it, "There are more movies here than in the video store back home in my village. And before you ask: yes, we still have video stores. Netflix has yet to conquer deepest, darkest Africa."

I looked over at my other friend who had offered to help me without a moment's hesitation. Still, given the way he'd been leering at the screen, part of me wondered if he was only here for the movies.

"Not true," Deirdre said, setting her hands at her sides—the fae equivalent of throwing a huff. "In Mag Mell I often rode a crystal dragon into battle. We'd ride high above the ground, using the clouds as cover before diving through the cotton mist and smiting—"

"—your enemy with your sword arm," Egya said, waving a dismissive hand. "You've told us that story at least four times since boarding this plane. Face it, girl: you're afraid of flying."

Deirdre sat motionless for a long moment and I knew the changeling well enough to know she was considering the Ghanaian's words carefully. "No," she finally said, "I am not afraid of flying. I am afraid of falling."

Way to self-reflect, my fae friend.

"Aren't we all, girl." Egya giggled obnoxiously loud, which was quite uncouth of him seeing as we were in first class. Then again, outside of one woman who'd sat all the way in the front row, we were the only people in first class, so there wasn't really anyone else to annoy.

Well, except me. And given Deirdre's downcast eyes, the changeling, too. And probably the woman up front. I take it back— there were plenty of people to annoy.

Not that Egya noticed or cared if he did. His eyes were firmly fixed to his pod's screen as his fingers danced across it, hunting for the next movie to watch.

"Ignore him," I said. "He's just jealous you rode a dragon in the first place."

"Just seething. Now if you'll excuse me, Dr. Strange awaits," Egya added before touching the screen and escaping into a CGI abyss.

I turned to Deirdre. "As I was saying, ignore him. Why don't we pass the time with a little entertainment, too?" I leaned over and as I did, the Amulet of Souol fell out of my blouse. I tucked it back in before tapping Deirdre's screen.

"Milady, the amulet. You brought it with you?" she said in surprise.

I ignored her, scrolling through the seemingly infinite list of movies.

"Are you not afraid someone will try to take it from you?"

I shook my head. "That's why I brought you. You're my anti-magical-amulet theft device."

"That I am!" she said, pounding a fist against her chest. "Still ..." Her voice trailed off as she formulated her thoughts. "The amulet, it answers your greatest question. The one that burns through every fiber of your being. You asked it to lead you to your soul." She pointed at my map that, for cosmic reasons I'd never understand, only I could see. Deirdre, despite not being able to see herself, completely believed me when I told her it was there. "And since every fiber of my being desires to serve you, perhaps I can ask the question of how I can best do so?"

I groaned. "Deirdre, we've been over this. You can help me, not *serve* me. And as for asking the amulet a question, I know your greatest desire is to help me. But you know that the amulet will only answer one question. Mine happened to be about my missing soul. And while today yours would be about helping me, it might change later. I want you to reserve your question for ..."—I searched for the words that would resonate with the changeling warrior—"an important mission of your own."

Deirdre's eyes glistened with unescaped tears. "You are too kind, milady. Of all the warriors I have served—"

"Uh, uh, uh," I said, wagging a scolding finger.

"Ahh, warriors I have *helped* ... none have been as generous as you." She pounded her chest again.

I gave Deirdre a nod and continued scrolling through her movies until I found something I thought she'd enjoy. I finally settled on *Pride and Prejudice and Zombies.*

I handed her the complimentary noise-cancelling Beats earphones. She resisted, but I pushed them onto her. "You are my friend, Deirdre. Not my charge or squire or whatever role you used to play in fae army heirarchy. And to that end ..."—I pressed play—"enjoy now, smite later."

The changeling nodded before finally putting them on.

↔

. . .

First class was normally my favorite place to be and even though I had been insistent on enjoying it, the truth was I couldn't really enjoy anything anymore.

Seems your soul is kind of instrumental to enjoyment. Without one, everything tasted flat, colors were muted and joy seemed capped just below the I'd-rather-be-anywhere-else threshold. It was like being severely depressed (and the GoneGods know I'd initially thought that was what was wrong with me).

I wasn't the depressed type. If I felt bad, I could generally shop it away. But there wasn't a pair of pumps in this world or any other that could lift my spirits and even though I'd only been like this for a few months, it was already costing me everything I loved.

My grades were suffering, my life was stalled and my boyfriend... Well, let's just say that my love life was in critical condition. It didn't help that Justin had just been possessed by a dybbuk demon I had accidentally exposed him to.

The result was that he didn't go home for Christmas break. Didn't go home and didn't call home to tell his parents, either. So they came up to find him and *that's* how I met my boyfriend's parents. With them worried half to death that their son had missed turkey dinner and fully blaming the new girlfriend for the ensuing worry.

Luckily, the dybbuk demon had been killed the day before. Thank the GoneGods for small miracles.

In the end, we made up some excuse about how we'd been fighting, with me falling on my sword in apology. Needless to say they hated me, giving me the we'll-never-accept-you death glare as they whisked him home for the rest of the holidays.

And as for Justin, given I was the one who had exposed him to the dybbuk demon in the first place, I doubted we were friends anymore ... break-up aside, of course.

But I couldn't think about any of that now because I was on a plane to Japan so I could seek my soul. I pulled back my left sleeve and looked at my forearm, where translucent lines of orange and blue rolled over my skin like the ocean rolling in on a white, sandy beach. And as the two colors ebbed and flowed, I saw lines that I recognized as a bird's eye view of the Ryukyu islands. Of course, that was its ancient name. Now, most referred to Ryukyu as Okinawa, the southernmost islands of Japan, a tropical paradise and the setting of *The Karate Kid*.

But besides an outline of the island, the magical map offered few additional details. I had hoped that as we flew closer to Japan it would change, do something—anything—other than this soft, constant shifting. *I guess I'll have to wait and see if anything changes when we land,* I thought.

"Milady?" Deirdre said, still watching her screen with utter fascination as Miss Elizabeth Bennet dispatched a zombie.

"Nothing," I muttered, really wishing my inner thoughts would stay *inner*.

I rolled down my sleeve, covering the map that apparently only I could see (despite both Deirdre and Egya doing all kinds of experiments on my arm that included, but weren't limited to: holding a magnifying glass over it, rubbing lemon and applying heat, pouring baking powder on it and a Ouija board séance.)

No matter what they did, nothing revealed the map to my soul. It seemed I was the only one who could see it. Why? I had no idea and could only think of one other person to ask: the Raspy Man. I didn't trust him. Hell, only weeks earlier he'd sent a hit man of sorts after me. But he was the only person who seemed to know anything about this subject.

But that had been a total waste of time. The Raspy Man didn't have a clue, simply wondering in that out-of-breath voice of his whether he could see it given that he, too, was missing his soul. I might have been a cute blonde (well, more an auburn than *blonde* blonde), but I was no fool.

Try to kill me once, shame on you. Try to kill me twice and its shame on me.

Regardless of who else could see the map, I could. And it clearly told me to go to Japan. More specifically, Okinawa. Seeing the outline of the tiny Pacific island appear on my arm had caused me to breathe both a sigh of relief and let a groan of despair. Oddly enough, both were for the exact same reason: I'd been there before.

I'd felt relieved that I would be searching in a familiar place. The groan had been because I had gone to Okinawa during World War II to … well … hunt. War zones were perfect hunting grounds for a vampire. Lots of blood and destruction, and when people went missing it was generally assumed they had been captured or killed by the enemy. You know, the kind of stuff vamps look for when shopping around for their next meal.

Going there would dredge up some terrible memories. Memories I'd have relished as a vampire, but as a human would only churn my stomach with disgust and shame.

I know, I know. I was a vampire then, just doing what vampires do. And I wasn't that person anymore—after all, I was human again. But still, I did a lot of messed up things there, even for a vampire.

I wasn't proud of my time in Okinawa. Well, that's not entirely true. I was proud of one thing I did there—maybe the only good thing I ever did as an evil, blood-drinking vampire.

That was a long time ago, I thought (in my head) and chased away the memories. Okinawa would be a different place and I briefly considered scouring a map of the island for clues, or reading up on the history and mythology, but I decided not to do any of that. I wanted to relax and enjoy this trip as best I could.

I wanted to try and find what little joy I could as I rode this metal dragon to Japan.

Just relax, I thought, grabbing my sleep mask.

If only I had closed my eyes before leaning back, then I wouldn't have seen the only other person in first class staring at me. The strange woman stood near an unoccupied toilet (as evidenced by the green sign to prevent us first-classers from making the long trip to a locked bathroom). She held a telephone receiver and scowled at me like I had just stolen the life vest from under my seat.

Again, I might have ignored her if it wasn't for the floating eyeballs hovering right next to her head.

2

PLEASE FASTEN YOUR SEATBELT, YOU'RE ABOUT TO GET PUNCHED

*J*apan is different from Montreal (and Scotland, for that matter) in so many ways it's virtually impossible to list them all. That said, when I spent a few years there, I divided those differences into what I called The Three Ds: dinner, dress and demons.

Dinner and dress boiled down to sushi and kimonos. But demons … well, the differences between Japanese demons and Western ones were staggering.

For one thing, the Japanese had way more demons than any other culture I knew. And although their demons were malevolent, they weren't necessarily evil, with many of them only existing to fulfill some esoteric purpose (like in the case of the azuki arai demon, who—I kid you not—exists solely to wash azuki beans), or they were the result of some flaw like greed, lust or gluttony.

In other words, they were strange. And few were stranger to me than the futakuchi-onna. From the front, they looked like perfectly normal women—it was seeing them from behind that made things weird.

For one thing, their hair behaved more like tentacles than normal, dead cells growing out of your head should behave. For another, each had a large, almost human-looking mouth right on the back of their head. Despite all that, I found them relatively harmless except for their insatiable appetites. Invite them over for dinner and they were likely to eat anything and everything edible in your house, including your pet gerbil.

This futakuchi-onna wore a red headscarf that complemented her black shirt and skirt. The scarf covered up her demon-ness, presumably so as not to scare the human Nippon Airlines passengers. That in and of itself was odd, because Japanese folklore and myths were such a part of everyday life that when the gods left, the Japanese took a far healthier path to dealing with Others than the rest of the world: they adopted them as citizens almost immediately.

They even had their own name for Others: Kakureta no Kokujin, or Hidden Citizens. So this first-class passenger being a Japanese demon wasn't all that surprising.

But her hiding it? That was.

I would never have known she was an Other if it wasn't for her hair-tentacles wiggling out from under the scarf. Well, that and her two floating eyeballs that popped up like a pair of high-tech drones. The eyes were mokumokuren—spirits who usually live in torn shoji (paper sliding doors common in Japan)—but these two were just floating around like bees. (And like bees, I wondered if they knew that they weren't aerodynamic enough to fly.)

The floating eyeballs stared at my now covered arm like they had x-ray vision (which, for all I knew, they did). The way they fixated on my arm scared me. What's more, the futakuchi-onna dropped the phone as her hair slithered up to open the overhead compartment and retrieve a long cloth satchel.

She dropped the cloth to the ground, revealing what looked like the head of a spear that wasn't attached to any shaft. Shaftless spearhead or not, I didn't hesitate, rushing up to the front of the first class cabin and pushing her into the bathroom—minus her floating eyes.

↔

. . .

We tumbled into the unoccupied bathroom, where she fell on the toilet with a crash, the momentum of my tackle causing the door to slam behind us. Because it was first class, the bathroom was large enough for us both to be inside and have a wee bit of room between us. Not that I wanted any space between us for her to swing her spearhead.

I kneed her in the chest and slapped hard at her spear-holding wrist. She dropped her spearhead as she crashed—at least one thing was working in my favor—and I used my knee and hands to pin her body down on the metal toilet.

"*Gaijin,* what are you doing?" she said, her Japanese accent attaching an *uh* to the *g* in "doing."

" *'Gaijin?'* Seriously? We're over international waters, so you're just as much a foreigner here as I am. And as for what I'm doing, I could ask you the same thing. Last I checked it's impolite to attack fellow travelers with sharp things."

The two eyes now hovered near me—either they had found another way into the bathroom or they ghosted through the door. However they got in, they eerily examined my arm like undersea drones did a wreckage. Apparently they were completely unconcerned that I was in the middle of a fight. I swatted one away like a fly at a picnic.

"The mokumokuren ..."—the futakuchi-onna was also staring at my covered arm—"they see your map. You have a path to the Kami Subete Hakubutsukan."

"My Kami Subete Hakubutsukan?" I said, pulling back my sleeve. "You mean this?" I showed her my forearm. Her eyes widened as she looked at my exposed flesh. The two eyes floated in for a closer look. They reminded me of underwater videos where remote-controlled submarines examine sunken ships with spotlights. "You can see this?"

The futakuchi-onna nodded. "So it is true what he said. There is a seeker." One of the eyeballs floated closer to her. If they were communicating I couldn't hear it, but from the way her own eyes registered surprise, there was no doubt that the eyeball had told her something. "You—you are the one who donated her soul."

"I wouldn't call it a 'donation.' More like a forced deposit, or—"

There was a knock on the door. "Milady, is all well?"

"Yeah, girl," called Egya. "That was kind of a rushed dash to the bathroom. You eat something funny?"

Apparently they hadn't seen me tackle the futakuchi-onna—not that I cared. This futakuchi-onna knew something I didn't.

"He told me that you would come, but I didn't believe him."

"Who?" I repeated. "Who are you talking about?"

There was another knock on the door, this time the stewardess. "Excuse me, Ms. Darling. Your friends here tell me you are having trouble. I could ask for a doctor—"

"No doctor. I'm fine. I just need a minute to—"

But before I could say the last word, she pulled the spearhead into her hand with such speed that I barely had a second to push myself back and out of the bathroom. Stupid me ... I was so fixated on her that I forgot about her tentacle hair. Never, ever forget about the tentacles. That's Monster Fighting 101.

Stupid, stupid, stupid!

She pushed the spearhead through my abdomen and I screamed in pain. "Please," she said, "accept this gift."

"Gift," I huffed as I stared at the dangling spearhead in my chest. "Hell ... of ... a ... gift."

The head went right through me. I'd stabbed enough people in my time to know that this was a wound I wasn't recovering from. There wasn't a doctor in the world that could get this thing out of me and keep me breathing. "Stupid," I muttered to myself again.

"I—I didn't think he spoke the truth," she said, a tear falling from her eye as she turned around as if ashamed to look at me. Then, as if reciting a passage from some ancient tome, she uttered, "Dawn shall come when the sun sets on this world."

It seemed only her front face was ashamed, because her other mouth—the one on the back of her head—spat out venomously, "They want the map, but you cannot give it to them. You must come and claim your soul before it is too late. Failure will bring ruin to this world and the next."

" '*They*' want the map, but '*he*' doesn't want '*they*' to have it, huh? How very specific of you," I said, my hands still cupping my bloody wound. "If you're so desperate for me to go get my soul, maybe you shouldn't have stabbed me."

"But we did not," the futakuchi-onna answered. "We only—" But before she could finish, the bathroom opened. Evidently the stewardess had used some sort of key or latch to get in.

I fell flat on my back, and looking straight up at the stewardess, I waited for the requisite scream as I bloodied the first-class carpet. But she didn't scream; she just looked at me with disdain before glancing into the bathroom with equal disgust.

I reached for where the spearhead should have been sticking out of me, but my hands passed through empty air. I lifted my head; no metal tip in me. I looked in the bathroom. No futakuchi-onna, no mokumokure.

"Are you alright, Ms. Darling?" the stewardess said, no longer hiding her disdain.

"Yes, I think so."

"And?" the stewardess said, her arms akimbo.

"Umm, sorry for the trouble?" I offered from my horizontal position on the floor.

How embarrassing.

3

RESURRECTING THE DEAD—
GODDAMN STYLE

The stewardess looked at the mess in the bathroom and shook her head. "Is there anything I can help you with, Ms. Darling?"

Yes, I thought, *I've just been stabbed in the chest by a magically disappearing futakuchi-onna and her floating eyeballs. Best first-class gift I've ever gotten.*

Thankfully I hadn't thought that out loud; I'd probably end up strapped into my fancy pod for the rest of the flight.

I shook my head, still looking in the empty bathroom stall. "No," I said. "Just a nervous traveler, that's all."

The stewardess gave me an unsurprised look. "You'd be surprised how many of our first-class customers are nervous flyers." I could sense that she was using every ounce of her rapidly depleting willpower to avoid yelling at me.

I guess dealing with first-class brats must be factored into the ticket price.

"Sorry," I said.

"Very well, Ms. Darling. If there is anything you need, please do not hesitate to ask. Perhaps with my aid we can avoid further messes," she said with a curt bow before walking away.

She still wasn't out of earshot when Egya burst into laughter. "Girl, you are a strange one," he said between cackles. "A very strange one indeed."

Deirdre, on the other hand, did not laugh, presumably because she was worried about me. The changeling was always worried about me —in an endearing way (most of the time).

Now wasn't one of those times.

Before I could tell the overprotective changeling warrior that I was OK, she pushed past me into the bathroom and picked something off the floor.

She turned around, revealing a tiny seashell in her palm. She stared at it with awe and something that I rarely saw in the fae: Fear.

"Was this always here?"

↔

We returned to our pods, and in a hushed whisper I told them my story. Neither of them had seen the futakuchi-onna or the floating eyeballs. From their perspective, I was sitting perfectly calm in my seat and then I was charging to the bathroom like I had a fire in my pants.

Given that Egya thought I was having stomach issues, that description was quite literal—from the Ghanaian's perspective, at least.

Still, despite not seeing the creature themselves, they had been around the supernatural block enough times to believe me.

"So," Egya said, "you were attacked by a ghost. Mid-flight. In first class."

"Well, 'attacked' may not be the right word. I kind of tackled her before she got a chance," I said before shaking my head. Something was very wrong about all this. "And I'm not sure 'ghost' is the right word, either. I mean, she was an Other, and Others aren't ghosts."

"Ghosts are real," Egya said.

"They are, but the rules have changed. For one thing, since the gods left and took their magic, all ghosts have manifested and they are unable to use their magic to stay hidden anymore."

Egya shook his head. "That's not true. They can still use their magic, but it costs them time. They'd burn out pretty quick."

I nodded. Since the gods left, magic was in limited supply and any creature able to cast a spell could only do so by sacrificing life in exchange. They would have to burn their life away, shortening the time they had left on Earth by hours, days—sometimes even months—in exchange for the spell's effects.

And ghosts were particularly penalized for doing their typical now-I'm-here, now-I'm-not trick. No ghost in her right mind would burn so much time just to be invisible.

As if reading my mind (or maybe I was thinking out loud again), Egya asked, "Was she burning time? As you fought, did she show any signs of aging?"

I thought back to the skinny futakuchi-onna. Her face had been pale and she looked like she'd seen better days, but there were no visible signs that she was aging. "No," I said, and then I looked at my ridiculously expensive Jaeger-LeCoultre wrist watch checking if it had sped up. "What time do you have?"

Egya showed me his watch; our times matched. That was another thing about burning time: clocks sped up when near burnt time. "That confirms it—no magic," I said. "And even if there was, something's not right. A futakuchi-onna is a demon. An Other. But this one acted more like a ghost than a demon. Unless I'm mistaken, ghosts are the manifested representation of a human's soul. Others don't have souls, so they can't be ghosts."

"That is not entirely true," Deirdre said, speaking for the first time since we'd sat down. She moved the shell with her finger, turning it over and over. "Others might not have souls, but there are still ways for us to return to a living plane of existence. But I didn't think this kind of magic existed anymore." She paused before correcting herself. "*Could* exist anymore."

"You mean since the gods left?"

Deirdre shook her head. "No. This kind of magic was destroyed by the gods long before they left."

↔

"What kind of magic are we talking about? And what's up with you and that shell?"

Deirdre turned it over again, using her pinky finger to point out a tiny carving on the inside of the shell's concave surface before handing it to me. The carving looked like Celtic runes.

"*Middle* and *raise*," Deirdre said pointing to each symbol. "It refers to an ancient magic where a dead Other would be resurrected, but not fully. Half of their essence would remain in the Land of the Dead."

And she wasn't talking about the George Romero movie. The Land of the Dead was a place that so many ancient cultures included in their mythologies and legends. This was a *physical* realm mortals could visit, a la Orpheus when he was trying to rescue his wife, Eurydice.

"So she was partially brought back to life," I said. "What's the big deal about that?" In a world of angels and demons, dragons and yokai, ex-vamps and ex-weres, resurrection wasn't a big deal.

Sheesh, I thought, *talk about desensitization.*

"Only that the magic necessary to resurrect an Other, even partly, was closed away long ago." She twisted her hand like she was bolting a door. "*Locked* away long ago, when the gods negotiated the dominion of Death with the Thrones of Heaven."

"Thrones of Heaven? Which heaven?"

"*Heaven*, Heaven. The one shared by Yahweh, Allah and God."

"As in, capital *g*?" I gave her my best East Coast gang sign, which given my addiction to cocktails with tiny umbrellas, didn't really come off very gangsta.

Not that Deirdre even noticed my wee joke. "Before the gods left, when an Other died they ceased to be, but their essence remained behind like a hibernating bear in an eternal winter. Only great magic could wake such a slumber."

"Resurrection magic?" I asked.

Deirdre nodded. "Back when the Morrigan walked amongst us, we could be brought back to life if she ordained us worthy of a second life. Not that the Great Queen restored many of us—she saw our deaths as failure and the Great Queen was not one for second chances. But should we be deemed worthy or possess knowledge or power needed for her many conquests, she would find our essence and imbue it once more with life.

"But of all the Death gods, the Morrigan was the only one who possessed such power. A power that she—wisely—used sparingly. Until the great war, when the feathered serpent Quetzalcoatl died. His brothers and sisters came to the Morrigan, requesting she use her resurrection magic to bring the Aztec god back to life. My queen refused."

"Why?" I asked.

Deirdre shook her head. "It was not the place of a changeling warrior to question the decisions of her gods. We only served in their army. And for the next thousand years I served, fighting off the hordes of Aztec beasts, repelling them from our lands. A thousand years until the Under Heaven Accords were held.

"It was then that the Angels of God negotiated peace between our domains and one stipulation was set in place: no more resurrections of gods or Others."

"What about Jesus?" Egya asked.

"The Accords were thirty years after his resurrection and he was the last divine being to ever breathe life again after it was taken away."

"So gods can die, huh?" I said. "What does that have to do with our Other ghost?"

"An Other who was a ghost could not come back unless the Morrigan granted them life again. But when she did, the half-raised often carried an item with those two symbols on it." She pointed at the shell.

"So that shell was the futakuchi-onna's essence?"

"These runes give me cause to believe so," Deirdre said.

"And I killed her … again?"

Deirdre nodded.

I thought about what Deirdre had said. If she was right—and I had no way to know one way or another if she was—then some ancient power was being used to bring dead Others back to life. Well, to half-life, at least.

"Deirdre," I said, "you refer to the Morrigan as the Other capable of resurrecting an Other. The Morrigan, the Great Queen—as in a 'she.' But the futakuchi-onna kept talking about a 'he.' Any idea who that 'he' might be?"

"No milady, I do not."

"OK," I said, not sharing my own theory that this "he" might actually be the Raspy Man. My creepy stalker was the one who had told me that my soul was missing in the first place. He'd told me about the amulet and had been pulling strings along the way to get me to go after it. He knew things. Enough to bring a futakuchi-onna back to life? I doubted it, but then again, I wasn't sure what he was capable of.

Not that I mentioned him to either Deirdre or Egya. It wasn't that I didn't trust them—I trusted both of them with my life—but somehow every time I tried to bring him up, the words wouldn't come. Maybe I was afraid they'd make me stop talking to him and … well, he was the only person who truly understood what it meant to lose a soul, and part of me needed to speak to him.

But just because I doubted the Raspy Man had the power to ghost-ify an Other didn't mean that he was off the betrayal hook. After all, the futakuchi-onna's ghost had been waiting for me. Someone had to have told her where I'd be, and since I was pretty sure the Raspy Man had me under surveillance, that made him suspect numero uno.

I shook away those thoughts and turned to Deirdre. "Do you really think the Morrigan has returned?"

Deirdre shrugged. "I do not think so. She was a god and must have left with the other gods during the GrandExodus. She must have, for the Morrigan was not one to hide in shadows."

"But someone else could be using her trick, right?"

Deirdre raised a hand. "Perhaps, but such power is magnificent and I have not known the other gods to show restraint when it comes to exercising such power. If another god had the knowledge, then another god would have surely used it before now."

I had to hand it to the changeling: she made an excellent point. Gods weren't exactly the "holding back" type. If they had access to power, they'd use it.

And then there was one more thing to consider: what Ankou, a fae reaper, had told me three days earlier. Long story short, I had helped Ankou undo a great wrong and as a "reward," he warned me that powerful Others would want to claim my lost soul.

Why? Because apparently human souls were what powered divine domains. Think of them as the nuclear power plants to Heaven's streetlights. Without an active, fully operational plant, there'd be no lights in Heaven.

Seemed that Ankou was right about peeps wanting my soul. The only thing he got wrong was that those peeps just might be some god who forgot to get on the departing bus with the rest of them.

Oh hell, I thought, shaking my head as the idea of being in the crosshairs of a divine being dawned on me.

"Precisely. If the Morrigan has returned, then Hell is exactly what she seeks. She will try to reopen her domain."

"Oh girl," Egya said with a sneer, "nothing is ever easy with you, is it?"

No, nothing ever is.

4

COSTUMES, TAXIS AND JAPANESE MALLS

As we landed at Okinawa's Naha Airport, I tried to put what Deirdre had said out of my mind. We had no idea whether she was right. She was, after all, basing her entire theory on a seashell.

Still, the changeling was privy to ancient knowledge, and who knows what was in the plans of the gods.

We stood in line with multiple welcome and New Year's signs in just about every living language around us, including Elvish and Angelic. The immigration line had more Others than humans (which was unusual, even for a place as tolerant as Japan). So much so that I wondered if there was a Groupon for Others or something.

We were standing behind a large yeti—as in, the abominable snowman—wearing what can only be described as a baby blue, king-sized blanket with the logo of the Toronto Blue Jays printed all over it. I guessed he was trying to fit in by wearing an impromptu muumuu.

There were two things strange about that. One, yetis generally walked around naked, their fur hiding the places Adam covered with a fig leaf. And two, they didn't usually travel, instead spending their time in the forested regions of northern Canada.

To see one so far away from home was unusual. And if wearing a bed sheet wasn't strange enough, the yeti also wore a silver hoop around his neck that looked like a loop with several evenly spaced spheres around it. Each sphere was silver except for the bottommost, which was red, larger than the rest and had three Japanese kanji etched on it: *Sun, Heaven* and *Fields.*

I must have been staring too long because the yeti turned around and looked directly down at me. I'm five feet plus a hair. The yeti would have been my height if there had been a second me sitting on my shoulders.

"Go Blue Jays?" I said.

For a moment I thought he was going to bite my head off with his bear-like mouth, but instead he gave me a wide grin, revealing two rows of serrated teeth. "Sadly this is not their season—not that many seasons are these days."

I nodded in agreement, but the truth was, I had no idea. Baseball had always seemed impossibly slow to me, even when I was immortal and had all the time in the world to waste. "Nice necklace," I said.

He touched the hoop. "In this plane of existence, the planets rotate around the sun, never touching it, never getting closer to it. But the celestial bodies are different, for each one takes its turn touching their sun."

"And by celestial bodies, you mean the heavens and hells?"

The yeti nodded. "The gods' domains never stayed in one place, always moving along their own orbital path. But they did intersect in one place. Here." He touched the red sphere. Holding it still, he rotated the hoop so that another silver sphere entered into the red one. "They took turns residing in the sun."

"Humph," I said. "Thank the GoneGods our orbital path doesn't do that, or we'd all be one sunburn away from oblivion."

The yeti smiled. "In the world of the divine, a sun isn't always a sun."

"OK, now you're just getting weird."

"I'm a mythical creature of the forest. Weird is what I do." He stuck out his hand. "The name's Harry."

"As in *Harry and the Hendersons?*"

He nodded. "My yeti name is seventy-three letters long and diffi-cult for my own people to pronounce. Besides, I love John Lithgow."

"Me too," I said taking Harry's hand. "Kat. Kat Darling."

↔

We passed through Japanese customs without incident, despite Egya's constant bowing, ear-to-ear grinning and general annoyingness. Collecting our bags from the conveyor belts, I exchanged email addresses with Harry, who said he had a tour to catch and that we'd speak when we both got back to Canada.

With that done, we jumped into a taxi and got to the hotel without any more spear-wielding ghosts trying to kill us. Well, kill *me*. The futakuchi-onna really didn't seem interested in Egya or Deirdre. Lucky me.

We arrived at the Naha Terrace in downtown Naha—Okinawa's capital city—and once I was alone in my room, I looked at my arm again. The map was still zoomed out, showing me the whole island and its southern islands.

Damn it, I thought. I had hoped now that we were closer it would give me a few more details about where to look.

But just because I had an uncooperative magical map didn't mean I was out of options. This was an old stomping ground of mine (the stomping part being more literal than I would have liked) and I knew a couple folks who might be of use.

↔

I have an eidetic memory and contrary to what most believe, that doesn't mean I remember everything perfectly. What I can actually do is project images of what I've seen or experienced and replay that memory with near perfect recollection. It takes a few seconds to do, sometimes longer, and can be disorientating.

So when we went to the heart of Naha's downtown, Kokusai Dori, I was immediately thrown off by all the changes that came with modernization. I mean, when I first visited this place decades ago, not only was it during an era predating tall, concrete buildings and neon lights, but it was also during the middle of a war and the city had been razed to the ground by a typhoon of steel.

The U.S. military had bombarded this place with missiles shot from the safety of their ships, literally showering the land with so many shells that unexploded bombs were frequently found on the island to this day.

That and all the ridiculous streamers and paper lamps and signs celebrating New Year's threw me way off. As I tried to overlay my memory of this place, I found that almost nothing of what I remembered remained.

But "almost nothing" isn't nothing and after wandering up and down the streets, I saw a stone marker no longer than a pack of cards hidden at the corner of an alley. On it, a symbol that looked like a capital *t* with a line jutting out of its right side that pointed to the ground.

Shi Ta.

That meant "under."

↔

Downtown had paved roads with standard, concrete, block-like buildings, neon signs and a Starbucks. In other words, it was modern. But the alley wasn't ... but rather was a place seemingly frozen in the past. Single-story buildings with straw-thatched roofs lined both sides of the road, their edges hung with kanji-etched shingles that declared what awaited visitors inside.

What's more, Others of questionable repute stood outside many of the doors. And by questionable repute, I didn't mean that the rokuro kubi, azuki arai and shirime were questionable because of what they were, but rather because of what they did.

"Woah," Egya said, smiling at an azuki arai who pulled at her shirt's hem to reveal a bit more skin, "it is like we've traveled back in time."

"We have. Sort of," I said as a Japanese human stumbled out of a bar wearing a huge smile, obviously satisfied by the special Other attention he'd just gotten. "Before the gods left, this was 'Shita no Kami' ... Under the Gods. It was a hidden red-light district of sorts, and where I hung out between hunts."

"Hunts?"

I gave Egya a look.

Egya nodded cautiously. "Hunts. Got it."

We walked through the darkened alleys of Okinawa's Other world, passing by izakayas and snack bars. Despite this obviously being a poorer area, I was amazed by how clean it was. No litter or passed out vagrants or random streams of questionable liquids.

Very different indeed.

"Anyway," I said, pointing at three businessmen as they walked in our direction, "seems that when the gods left, this place ceased being hidden, but didn't cease being red-light."

"Milady," Deirdre said, "what are we doing here? Certainly this place is beneath you."

Which was ironic given Deirdre's liberal attitude toward clothing and, well ... naughtiness. In fact, just a few weeks ago she'd made a strange and quickly declined offer to "aid" Justin and me in bed.

And now I was thinking about Justin again, which would have sent a pang through my heart if I still felt things deeply. And the knowledge that I *should* feel a pang but didn't was even worse.

I shook my head to clear it. Back to the more urgent issue: feeling things and the necessity of regaining that ability.

"Thank you for saying so," I said, "but this place is exactly where I belonged back when I was—you know." I put two fingers where my fangs had once been. "Anyway, we're here because we're looking for an old … ahh … friend. If anyone knows where this map is pointing, it'll be him," I said as we made our way deeper into Under the Gods.

We walked for another few minutes until we found a building with a picture of a mouth on both sides of the door. "Good," I said, "it's still here, which means Kenji's still here."

"Who?" Egya asked.

"Kenji—my friend who's a wall," I said.

Egya cocked his head to one side, confused.

"Don't ask," I said, putting my hand on the door. "And remember, we're trying to be inconspicuous. Stealth is the word of the day."

↔

We walked in and the first thing I saw was a large, blown-up, black and white photograph of … well, me.

5

YOU MAY BE A NO ONE, BUT HERE
YOU'RE FAMOUS

*H*ere I was trying to fly under the radar, hide in the shadows, go unnoticed, and the first thing I see is a super huge photograph of *moi* right in the entrance for all to see.

Granted, the photo was old and in out-of-focus shades of gray, but it was clearly me. And not only was it me, I was standing in a field, holding the hand of a little girl whom I hadn't thought of for years. We were standing next to a wall about two meters high by one-and-a-half meters wide. That doesn't sound like a strange detail, except we were on a beach. As in, feet wet, sand and a beach at low tide. The wall stood out like a sore thumb ... or sore wall?

But that was Kenji; the nurikabe was always doing stuff like that.

In the picture, Blue was holding my hand in the way little kids do when scared: with their chins tucked into their shoulder, as close as they can get to their caretaker, no smile.

And of course it was at night. I was still a vampire, so long walks at sunset weren't really my thing.

I stepped closer to the photo to get a better look at the child. Even with its grainy finish, I could still see the features of the child, the only human who had ever made me feel anything as a vampire. And even now, with my soul gone and my feeling dampened by it not being around, I felt something stir deep inside me. That was what Blue did to you: she made you feel alive.

She was the little girl I'd saved all those years ago—the one good thing I did during my entire life as a vampire. The one act I could point to on Judgement Day (should it ever come) and say, "Hey, I wasn't all bad."

I stared at the picture, humbled that Kenji would hang such a memento for all these years and wondering where Blue was now. She was eight in the picture, but that was decades ago. Given that she was human, and as far as I knew had remained human throughout her life, that would put her somewhere in her eighties.

Deirdre set a hand on my shoulder. "Is that you?"

"Of course it is," Egya said. "Who else but our Katrina Darling would wear stilettos on a battlefield?"

I shook my head, turning to face them. "Look, mum's the word, OK?"

"I think our sneaky ninja plans may have been short-lived," Egya said, pointing behind me.

An onryo and ittan momen stared at me with wide, shocked eyes.

The onryo bowed several times in an overtly excited manner as she scurried past us like she needed to be somewhere else fast.

As for the ittan momen, he bowed before saying, "Katto Darulingu, you honor us with your presence. I shall summon Kenji-sama at once. The Obstructer of Ways will be so happy you are here. Please, please." He pointed into the izakaya, which the three of us entered.

↔

The izakaya was exactly as I remembered it: tatami mats and low tables. Exactly what you'd expect from a place like this, and I realized that Kenji kept this place as normal as possible (well, normal for the

GoneGod world that is; there were several tengues drinking saki through their long red noses).

There was nothing magical or particularly *Other* about the place. Patrons sat on the floor eating small dishes of yakiniku, tako, edamame and a dozen other dishes that such places provided. Think of it as the Japanese version of tapas, or mezza. Little plates of bite-sized food.

The walls were made of three-inch-wide planks of wood and hung with paintings of *Girl Diver and Octopuses* and *The Tale of Genji Scroll*, as well as photos of—I'm guessing—famous patrons, not that I recognized any of them. There were also two shisa statues standing on the shelf behind the cash register. They symbolized guardian dogs (if a dog was the size of a lion, only stronger, faster and more vicious) who protected those in their care from evil.

One sat with its mouth open as it "ate" evil. The other had its mouth closed to hold the evil in.

I'd been on the receiving end of an attack from a pair of shisa once in my life, and by the GoneGods if I never met another pair again, I'd consider it a life well-spent. I breathed a sigh of relief that these two were just statues.

The only difference between the izakaya I remembered and the one I stood in now was that, among the Others heartily drinking their beer and sake sat several humans, one of whom was an American. Argh.

↔

The American walked up to me with a smile that looked all the more sleazy given he was wearing what looked like a Hawaiian shirt.

Still, despite his Larry the Lounge Lizard stride, he was cute. For an older guy.

Egya, seeing that I was about to be hit on, steered Deirdre away so the changeling wouldn't come to my rescue. Egya was always hunting for the laugh, and I could just see how this one would play out: *"Remember the time you were looking for your soul and this American guy hit on you ..."*

"Hello," the American said, giving me a big smile.

Even though he was wearing a ridiculous shirt, if you looked at him from just the neck up, he was cute. Shallow dimples, a big inviting smile, short black hair. If he had longer hair he'd look a bit like Justin, and—

The thought of my boyfriend hurt my heart and suddenly I went from warming to the possibility of a wee bit of flirting to Arctic cold.

I didn't answer.

"Hello," he repeated, sticking out his hand, "I'm—"

"Not interested," I said.

"OK," he said, "if you're not interested in my name, no harm. I'll just have to forego the introduction. From henceforth, please refer to me as 'You' or 'That guy,' or—"

"Funny," I said. "Must work wonders." I wondered if he recognized me from the photo in the doorway. Probably not. As a human, he wouldn't think I was the subject of a photo taken decades ago. Besides, even if he did recognize me, what did it matter? He was some stupid human—none of my concern.

"If by 'wonders' you mean getting my ass kicked a lot, then yes, I am a fountain of miracles."

Damn it, cute *and* funny. My Achilles heel.

"Look, I'm flattered, but you're a little old for me," I said, hoping a blow to his ego would send him packing.

"Old?" he said, putting a hand on his chest as if my word was a bullet that had hit him. "I'm twenty-four. How young do you want them? Besides,"—he lifted his hand; a silver ring hugged the base of his left ring finger—"And happily," he added.

"Humph," I said. "Can't be that happy if you're here and she's ... where?"

"Back home," he said, keeping it vague. "Look, I know you're cute.

You know you're cute. But I'm not looking for a hook-up, believe me. It's just that this is a bit of a rough place and—"

"You're trying to protect me? In that shirt?"

"It's kariyushi-wear, traditional for these parts." He looked down at his shirt. "It's what people wear here. And yes, I'm trying to protect you—by asking you to leave. We wouldn't want a tourist to like you to get hurt because you wandered off the beaten path and—"

"Ms. Darling, it is truly an honor to meet you again." An oni demon with a metal ring the size of a frisbee in his tusk bowed deeply in my direction. "My master wishes your company," he said, pointing to the beaded room at the back of the izakaya.

As I walked toward the curtains, I turned to the kariyushi-wearing man and winked. "Whatever will a tourist like me do?"

6

WALLS, WALLS AND MORE WALLS

*A*s the oni demon led me to the back, I motioned for Egya and
Deirdre to wait for me here—a request about which Deirdre
was not happy. I heard a small "milady" of protest behind me, and I
made an it'll-be-fine gesture at her before I stepped away.

At least, I was pretty sure it would be fine.

The demon escorted me through a beaded curtain and into a
secluded room before bowing deeply and leaving.

To an untrained eye this room looked empty. It had no exit, only
one chair and four—if you counted the entrance—identical walls with
nothing on them. But my eyes weren't untrained.

I approached the three walls and examined them more closely
before picking the one to the right and running my fingers over it in a
tickling fashion. "Come on, Kenji," I said as I tickled the wall. "Come
out, come out wherever you are."

The wall ceased to be a solid, boring piece of wood and turned
into a convulsing structure that roared with laughter. *"Yamite. Yamite,
kudosai,"* it said between chortles.

"You want me to stop, huh?" I giggled. "Then you'll have to say the
magic word."

"Wordo?" it said between struggling breaths.

"Come on. You remember, don't you?"

The wall got its laughter under control as it thought. Finally it spoke in a heavy Japanese accent. *"Penappuru."*

The Japanese alphabet was nothing like the English one. For one thing, with the exception of the letter *n*, every consonant had to be coupled with a vowel. Letters like *h* had five distinct sounds to them: ha, he, hi, ho and hu. And unlike English, where the vowels *e* or *i* could have multiple pronunciations, theirs only had one. The letter *e*, for example, was pronounced with a sharp *a* sound, and the letter *i* was a sharp *e*. In other words, the word "hi" in Japanese would be read as the English word "he."

Then get rid of the letter *l* and you'd know exactly three percent of what you need to know to speak Japanese.

I worked through the word *penappuru* … "Pineapple. Very good," I said, stopping my tickle onslaught. "Safety word activated. How are you doing, my old friend?"

The wall crackled, its wooden exterior taking on more of a skin-like quality before it shuffled away from the real, non-living wall behind it. "I am doing well," it said in an accent more natural to an English speaker, but still distinctly Japanese. I guess it's hard to enunciate when you're being tickle-tortured. "I am so happy to see you again, Katto. So very happy."

I looked up at the animated wall. "Me, too."

"But something is different about you," Kenji said, the wall crinkling as it spoke. (I only referred to Kenji as an "it" because it possessed no sex to speak of. Truth was, for all I knew Kenji was a "he" or "she." Then I had thoughts of planks of wooden walls piled at a hardware store and wondered if that was Kenji's version of an orgy. I shuddered at the thought).

Kenji was a nurikabe, one of the stranger Japanese Others. In the annals of Japanese myth, nurikabe were "Obstructers of Ways," placing themselves as false walls to confuse their victims or get them lost. But I found that, at least in Kenji's case, that bit of lore was just that. Kenji never turned us around, never tried to confuse us. If anything, it helped Blue and me by first saving our lives and then finding a home for Blue with the noro priestess.

But that was a lifetime ago. And now … well, now I was just happy to see my old friend after all these years.

"Different?" I said, repeating his question. "No, not really. Oh, there is this one thing, though. Hardly worth mentioning really, but I'm human again."

"Ahh, yes," the wall said. "So much magic gone now that the gods are no more. Half-breeds like you have lost their magic selves. Now they are all human. Too bad—I always liked werewolves. So much fun to play fetch with."

"And what about vampires? You never liked us?"

Kenji chuckled. "Most, no. One, yes." The wall bent over slightly in my direction, its way of pointing.

"So glad to have made the cut," I said.

"Are you here to see Blue?"

"Blue-chan? She's still alive?" My voice took on a bit more anticipation than I'd intended.

"Yes," Kenji said, not missing it. "Alive, strong. Not so much a *chan* anymore," referring to the Japanese moniker reserved for the young. "She is old now."

"That's what happens when you're mortal."

"*Hai,*" he said. "We grow old. All of us."

"We all grow old these days. Old and gray," I agreed with the nurikabe, who currently looked like a plain wall. Kenji could change his appearance to look like any kind of wall he liked; right now he was wafer-thin and wooden, which I interpreted as letting his guard down. *So we're still friends after all,* I thought with a smile. "That's something we all have in common now," I said.

"She grew up well, Kat. She became one of the most respected noro priestesses on the Ryukyu islands."

That's good, I thought. When I left her with the priestesses, I wasn't sure if they'd take to her, given that she was being dropped off by a *gaijin yokai*—literal translation: foreign demon. But the mere fact that she became a noro priestess meant they had accepted her, and she had become a highly respected one, at that. Well, that was no surprise; Blue had more charisma than an archangel and a smile that infected you with joy.

"I could call her if you like," Kenji said, breaking me away from my thoughts. "I could call Blue. She doesn't live far from here."

I thought about it. It would be amazing to see Blue again (and I didn't care how old she was—she was still a *chan* to me). But I had left her after the war, placing her in the arms of loving, adoptive parents, and never came back. Sure, I'd set up a trust fund with enough money that she would never have to worry about being homeless again, but *I* never came back. I never called or wrote or did anything to let the little girl—now old woman—know I was alive.

I'd wanted her to have a normal life. You can't have a normal life when your fairy godmother is a vampire, and so I figured the best thing for her was for me to stay away.

When the gods left four years ago and I became human again, I didn't try to find her because I worried she might have died from old age or disease or whatever humans died from. The thought that she might be gone was too much to bear, so I lived content not to know. That way, I could at least pretend she was alive.

But now I had confirmation she was alive, and my heart beat with nervous, anxious anticipation at the thought of seeing her again.

Except I was here to find my soul, and I had already been attacked once by a half-dead Other. I was being hunted, which meant that anyone near me would also be hunted. I had spent the last several decades staying away to protect her and I wasn't about to selfishly put her in harm's way just because I wanted to see her again.

I shook my head. "No," I said. "Not now. It's too dangerous."

"*Abunai?*" Kenji asked.

I rolled back my sleeve and showed the wall my arm, which was strange because I had no idea if nurikabe even had eyes. "Please tell me you can see this, or sense it, or whatever you have that passes for sight."

The wall bent slightly and I placed my forearm in its crease. "I am sorry, but I cannot sense anything."

GoneGodDamn, I thought. "I had hoped you could. I figured you might be able to see it since you are the Obstructer of Ways. But I guess it makes sense. So far I'm the only one who can see it. Well, me and a weird futakuchi-onna who said it was a map to the Kami Subete Hakubutsukan."

"Kami Subete Hakubutsukan," Kenji said in a hushed voice. *"Abunai."*

Abunai meant dangerous. "Do you know what this is?"

Kenji paused for a long moment, growing so perfectly still it became hard for me to see Kenji as anything but a wall and not the living, breathing creature it was. Then an image appeared on Kenji's surface. It was another map and I took a mental snapshot of it.

"Not what—*where.*"

"This place?" I asked, touching the center of the map (not that Kenji could see me doing that). "This map isn't telling me much more than that it's somewhere in Okinawa."

A red dot appeared on the center of Kenji's map, about six inches above where I'd placed my finger. "It is legend that the Kami Subete Hakubutsukan is somewhere hidden on Kakusareta Taiyo Shima," the wall said before pausing. "Say, you aren't one of those—ahh, how do you say in English?—nut jobs screaming about the Three Who Are One, are you?"

"Three Who Are One?" I said. "Sounds like something that belongs in a *Harry Potter* novel."

Kenji chuckled before his voice took on an annoyed voice. "In the last six months we have many Others from all over the world come to our little island, claiming to be the Heralds of the Three Who Are One. I keep telling them that I don't know what Three Who Are One is, but they keep on coming in, asking the same question."

"Again, what is Three Who Are One?"

"An event? A person? Some messiah who will come back from the dead? I have no idea. All I do know is that they believe tomorrow night will usher it in, whatever it is."

"Tomorrow night? You mean New Year's Eve?" I said, not telling him about the Morrigan or my soul. Whatever the Three Who Are

One was, I wouldn't be surprised if it had something to do with either of those things.

"Ahh, but tomorrow isn't just any New Year's Eve. Tomorrow is special because it is also Celestial Solace. Think of it as the New Year's Eve for the gods, but it lasts three months. And every three hundred and thirteen years, their new year and the human new year overlap."

"I see. Kind of like a divine Y2K."

"Y2K?"

"You weren't mortal then. Big New Year's event. Everyone thought the world was going to end, except not really. Most of us took it as a joke, a fun little extra to put into that year's celebrations. But there were a few that took it very, very, very seriously."

"Ahh, then yes. A divine Y2K it is. And because we are dealing with mythical creatures whom superstition infects like a cancer, they are coming here and annoying me with questions I have no answers to. Don't they know that their superstitions should have left with the gods?" Kenji sighed. "So nothing to do with Three Who Are One *bakajin*, huh? OK, then what is it that you seek?"

I considered telling him about what had happened to me, about how I'd briefly turned into a vampire because of some powerful Other's spell, about how when I broke the spell and became human again, not all of me came back—that my soul did not return, but instead was captured in some jar or vase or whatever you keep souls in these days, somewhere in Okinawa.

But instead I pursed my lips and said nothing.

"Very well," Kenji said. "But tell me this: does the map show you where on the island the Kami Subete Hakubutsukan is?"

"No. Right now it's just a map of Okinawa. I had hoped when I landed here it would give me more details, but so far, nothing. That's why I came to you."

Kenji paused before leaning in, its wall-like body folding around me as though trying to encase me in a room of its own making. "There are those who would kill for this map."

"I know," I said. "One of them tried to kill me on the plane over.

But I don't know why. I have an idea—a theory, even, but nothing concrete. What is a Kami Subete Hakubutsukan anyway?"

The wall took in a deep breath. "*Hakubutsukan* means 'museum' and *Subete* means 'everything.'"

"The Museum of Everything?" I asked, sitting down for the first time since meeting my old wall friend. When I sat, I noticed three men in cheap business suits staring in my direction through the beaded curtain. Private room we may be in ... but secluded? Not as much as I would have liked.

The Japanese businessmen, or as they're affectionately referred to in Japan: salarymen—salary men—stared at us as if there was nothing more interesting in the world. *Not really that strange given I am a cute, auburn-haired gaijin in a seedy part of town,* I tried to convince myself as I chatted with Kenji. *They probably think I'm some kind of high-end call girl or something. After all, these salary men probably weren't here for a beer or three after work. They were looking for some Other extra-recreational activities.*

"Ahh, but that's where it gets complicated. *Kami* refers to the gods. So it's the Gods' Museum of Everything," Kenji said, drawing my attention away from them.

"Hold on. Are you telling me that the gods built a museum and that's what I'm looking for?"

The surface of Kenji's wall changed and I watched as images of gods appeared. And not just Japanese gods; we had Zeus represented by the lightning bolts in his hand, Odin with his one eye, Ganesha with his elephant head, Shiva with each of her many arms holding a different weapon. There was Enlil, Enki and Inanna, and Sheela Na Gigs and Isis. Every major and minor god appeared in succession.

Once Kenji had established the Who's Who of gods on its surface, it drew an image of a building not unlike the Smithsonian. One by one the gods moved to the building in a style of animation that reminded me of the old stop-motion cartoons, each step awkward and sudden. There I watched as the gods placed items in there. The Staff of The Monkey King, the Arc of the Covenant, the Lance of

Longinus (the spear that pierced Jesus's side), Odin's Eye, Izanami-no-Mikoto's comb. The list went on and on.

This continued for a while before the last god, Anubis, placed what looked like an urn in front of the museum's door. Then the building sucked everything in like quicksand before sinking into the ground and disappearing.

I thought McGill's Library of Other Studies had some interesting and rare, once-upon-a-time magical items. But this place was absolutely filled with items of rare and impossible power.

"The gods knew that items of such power, in mortal or immortal hands alike, would disrupt balance. That is why they shut it away forever."

"Then why call it a museum? And why give it a Japanese name?"

"It was the Japanese Shinto gods who built this place in Yomi, the Shinto afterlife," Kenji said, pausing as it considered my second question. "And as for it being a museum … they are well-guarded places, but they are also open. I believe the gods wanted all that power to be able to flow out while simultaneously confining the items themselves."

Makes sense, I thought. *After all, my soul needed a way into the Soul Jar. And when the gods left, they needed a way to let the souls out, if only that one time.*

"Soul?"

Damn it—I was thinking out loud again. I hadn't meant to tell Kenji what I was looking for. Not because I didn't trust the nurikabe, but because I didn't know how crazy the "he" who sent the futakuchi-onna after me was. For all I knew, "he" would torture my poor friend for information, so the less Kenji knew, the better.

That was the plan, at least, but my ridiculous thinking-out-loud mental illness had other plans.

Kenji shuffled another two steps in my direction. "Soul? But you are human now."

"I am. Look, it's a long story, but my soul has been taken and this map that only I can see says it's somewhere in Okinawa. I'm trying to —" I was leaning forward, looking around nervously as I spoke, and that's when I saw it. Right under the palm of one of those drab-

45

looking Japanese salarymen was a mokumokuren, its floating eye pointed in my direction.

"Kenji," I said as casually as I could, "you don't happen to have a sword that I could borrow, do you? There are a couple of ghosts I need to chop down."

End of Part 1

PART II
INTERMISSION

7

OKINAWA — WORLD WAR II

ecades Ago—

Learning Japanese was easy when you had a photographic memory and a team of teachers working with you around the clock. Teachers, I might add, who were motivated by me not eating them.

And that's exactly what I did (or didn't do, as it were). I stowed away on a Japanese fishing boat off the coast of Nago with the goal of making my way to Okinawa, the place where the heaviest fighting between the U.S. and Japan was taking place.

It was April 1945 and I'd heard that the war might be ending, so I was anxious to make my way there as soon as possible.

I wanted to hunt in a war zone—a vampire's paradise. A setting where bodies went missing all the time. A place where blood filled the air like pollen in a field of lavender during the spring.

It was on that ship that I motivated the sailors to teach me Japanese, a task they took on like their lives depended on it—because, well, they did.

We sailed for nine days before making our way to the little war zone where I disembarked, having not eaten a single one of them. They had, after all, successfully taught me Japanese, and even though I was an evil vampire, I still kept my word.

(Sadly, even though I didn't eat them, I heard that their ship was sunk by a U.S. destroyer. During the heaviest days of fighting, the Americans had decided that everyone not flying their star-spangled flag was an enemy.)

I took a deep breath on the shores of Okinawa and smelled exactly what I was looking for. Blood.

↔

The first few days were paradise, with soldiers everywhere. I'd follow an advancing troop and wait for a soldier to peel off to pee or take a rest or—more often than you'd think—attempt to desert their regiment.

They were my main meals.

And during the day, I found a deserted hut deep in the Okinawan rainforest where I could rest, mostly safe from the sun's deadly rays. The deserted hut was far enough inland that I didn't encounter a single soul for the first three weeks living there. That hut was my base of operations and I left it only to hunt at night.

I was totally isolated. Until I wasn't.

↔

One morning in late April, I heard footsteps. Waking from my slumber (for a vampire, I was a light sleeper), I peered outside my window and saw a Japanese soldier pulling a rope with three civilians bound to it at the wrists. I don't know why he was there; as far as I could sense, there wasn't another soldier anywhere nearby.

He tugged at the rope, pulling hard. The first one in the line was a child, and from the way the other two looked down at the kid, I knew they were her parents. The soldier pulled them toward the hut and for a moment I thought he was going to pull them inside.

Great, I thought, *food delivery*.

But he didn't pull them in, stopping about ten feet away from the hut. There he pulled out his pistol, and with about as much emotion as one might feel throwing away their trash, shot the two adults.

I was sure the little girl would scream, would try to run away. But the little human didn't. She just stared up at the soldier with hate-filled eyes. Some emotions have physical presence. Most can't feel it, but vampires, we're attuned to human feelings. We can hunt just by sensing fear and following it to the source. In that moment, I felt such a searing hate that I had to take a step back, lest I end up burned by it.

If the soldier felt her rage, he offered no indication. Instead he pointed his pistol at her. *"Sutorippu."*

Strip.

The bastard. Not only had he just killed her parents, but now he wanted to—

I might have been evil, but even I couldn't stand for such an ugly, disgustingly depraved act. I stepped into the threshold of the doorway and cried out, *"Yamite."* I couldn't go to him. It was daytime and I couldn't risk being burned by the rays of light that made their way through the trees' canopy.

The soldier turned around, and seeing an auburn-haired *gaijin* girl nearly floored him. Until, that was, he got it in his head that he could double his fun.

He took a step toward me. *Good*, I thought. *Come to me and let me show you all kinds of pain*.

The soldier didn't make it three steps before the little girl jumped on his back and, with bound hands, started hitting him.

The kid had a lot of heart. Unfortunately, she was just a kid and heart isn't strength. The soldier knocked her off and pointed his pistol at her. He intended to kill her now that he'd seen he could upgrade his perversion with me.

I burst out of the hut, risking the sun, and kicked him in the back of the knee. He went down and I was about to end him right then and there, but a ray of sun hit my shoulder and I fell back in pain.

The soldier turned around and seeing my skin searing, cried out, *"Akuma."* The devil.

I wasn't a devil. If I was, then the heat wouldn't hurt me. But as it stood, I was practically in flames.

He emptied his gun at me and the blows knocked me over, exposing more of my body to the quarter-sized beams of light breaking through the leaves. I don't think I've ever been in so much pain; the world started blurring as I began to pass out.

I was trying to crawl back when I heard the soldier scream. The last thing I saw before passing out was the little girl covering me with dirt and leaves.

↔

When I woke, it was dark and I was no longer covered in dirt. I sat up, still in pain from the gunshots and burns, and what I saw was nothing short of amazing.

The soldier lay on the ground, his knife sticking out of his neck. I could only guess that when he was distracted by shooting me, the little girl had stolen his knife and stabbed him in the neck. Smart girl —if she had stabbed him in the back or leg, it wouldn't have killed him. By going for the neck, she'd saved herself. And me.

She was standing over her parents' bodies, both buried under a pile of rocks. She got on her knees, muttering something between tear-filled prayers.

I sat up more and the girl stirred, staring in my direction. Again, I thought she'd run, but instead she bowed in my direction. *"Arigato."*

"You're welcome, kid," I said in English. "But your thanks may be short-lived." I sat up, cringing in pain. I was hurting and I knew that if I could only get to her and feed, the pain would go away.

I stood and made my way to her. "It's nothing personal, but I'm a creature of the night and you—well, you're my food. So if you don't mind …"

Then I did the one thing you never do as a vampire: I popped out my fangs. Stupid. You never do that unless you have your victim in your hands. That was Vampirism 101.

Looking back, I think I made that rookie mistake because I wanted her to run. I wanted to give her a fighting chance, maybe even the playing field. After all, she had saved me.

But whatever my unconscious motivations may have been, she didn't run. She didn't even express fear. She just looked at me with her big brown eyes and I sensed acceptance in her. She was prepared to die.

Kind of made sense. She had just lost her parents. She had just killed a man. These were events that tended to weigh on a human soul, and I wondered if she wanted to die.

But I had sensed the desire to die before, most often while hunting in desolate places where many welcomed death. This child wasn't one of them. If anything, she looked determined to go on. To live on. But she didn't run. Why?

I never learned the answer to that question and I never ate her, either. This child had a will of steel and I couldn't bring myself to be the one to rid the world of one such as her.

Besides, I still owed her one.

8

SHIT ... SHISA

*3*6 HOURS BEFORE THE NEW YEAR—

"A sword?" Kenji asked. "We keep a *daisho* behind the bar, but ..." Its voice trailed off as it picked up on my tone of voice. "I sense nothing."

"The three salarymen at the table. The ones who haven't had a drink since coming into this place," I said. "They have a mokumokuren with them just like the futakuchi-onna who attacked me on the plane."

In the izakaya, the mokumokuren was still staring at me through the beaded curtain. No—not at me. *At my arm.*

I stood up, preparing to make my move.

"Salarymen? There are no salarymen in my izakaya at this moment. And as for the mokumokuren, I do not sense its presence, either. A changeling and two humans, yes, but a mokumokuren, no."

I thought about that. "Can you sense the dead?"

"No," Kenji said. "I am one who helps or hinders the living."

It was starting to make sense. No one had seen the very real and physical (to me, at least) futakuchi-onna, and she had a floating eye.

54

Which meant that these guys were probably dead as well. But if they were anything like the ghost on the plane, then their deadness wouldn't do me much good. They could hurt me just like she had.

"Well," I said, moving my neck side to side to limber up. "There are three salarymen and a mokumokuren. My best guess is that they're dead and they're here to steal my map. My very-attached-to-my-skin map, at that."

"I don't know what you are talking about."

"You don't have to—you just have to trust me. Now, if you don't mind. The kanashibari behind the bar. What's his name?"

"Akira."

"Really?" I said, surprised.

"Yes."

"Humph, makes sense I guess. I just thought after the movie no one went by that name anymore. Anyway, wish me luck, Kenji."

"Luck?"

But before the wall could ask or say anything else, I burst through the beaded curtains and tumbled toward the bar. As I unfolded out of my somersault, I cried out, "Akira, *daisho imasugu kudasai.*"

The kanashibari looked up at me and, much to its credit, didn't hesitate as it reached behind the bar and threw me both the long and short samurai swords hidden behind the bar. I caught them, letting the momentum of the throw unsheathe them before lunging at the three ghosts.

The salarymen didn't have time to react before my swords went through them. And as the blades pierced their bodies, they disappeared until only the eye remained.

The eye gave me a grimace (which, for a floating eyeball, was pretty impressive), blinked twice and vanished.

"Booyah!" I cried out in triumph. I'd just dispatched three ghosts without even breaking a sweat. Pretty damn cool, if I said so myself. Too bad no one else could see the ghosts. As far as they were concerned, I'd just attacked air.

The American had been mid-sip, his beer paused at his lips. "Why do the cute ones always have to be the crazy ones?" he muttered.

Deirdre and Egya came to my side. "Milady," the warrior changeling said as she scanned the room for danger, "are we under attack?"

"More ghosts?" Egya asked.

"Yeah." I nodded.

Kenji shuffled out of the room, the beads making a light tapping sound that sounded like a hundred marbles hitting the ground. "Kat-to," he said, his heavy accent returning, *"baka janai?"*

"No, I'm not crazy. There really were three—"

But before I could finish my sentence, two hooded men stepped into the izakaya. "Kuso," Kenji said. "Heralds."

"Heralds?" I said, but before I could ask who these two monk-rejects were, they started chanting. And they weren't in tune.

Apparently that didn't matter, because two giant golems burst through the wall, followed by two animated shisa statues the size of mopeds.

Fan-friggin'-tastic, I thought. *There had to be shisa.*

9

AGYO AND UNGYO AND THEIR PET SHISA, OPEN AND CLOSED

As if shisa weren't bad enough, they were accompanied by two golems. Nio, to be exact. In other words, two huge, wrathful, muscular stone golems who usually hung out outside Buddhist temples as non-moving statues. Like the shisa statues, one had his mouth open, the other closed.

The open-mouthed one was called Agyo and he held a vajra in his hand. Think of a diamond-shaped mace, add in a dash of lightning magic and then think bigger than my head and you'll start to get an idea of what kind of weapon he wielded. His closed-mouthed companion was Ungyo, and he wielded a sword bigger than the one Mel Gibson used in *Braveheart*.

Yay.

"Tell me you can sense those," I said to Kenji.

From the way it shuffled back through the beaded curtain, I knew Kenji could. The nurikabe was making its escape, not that I blamed it —Kenji was a wall, not a fighter.

"Deirdre, Egya," I said as we squared off against the four guardian warriors, "let's get the civilians out of here." Not that I needed to say any of that. The bar had cleared out; the only straggler was an ashwang from Pilipino mythology. The ugly, bat-like creature looked at the nio and shisa and bowed before screaming in Tagalog, "Three Who Are One approach this night!" Once he'd had his drunken say, he too ran out the door.

The bar was empty except for Deirdre, Egya and myself ... oh, and the stupid American. For some reason he stayed behind, too.

Without looking at him, I said, "By civilians, I mean him." I pointed my sword in the American's direction.

I heard the unmistakable click of a shotgun. "Little Miss Sunshine, I'm many things, but a civilian is not one of them." And before I could say or do anything, he unloaded a round right at the open-mouthed shisa.

↔

A gun, even a shotgun, can't hurt a shisa golem. They're made of magical stone harder than diamond. Chip it, sure, but actually hurt it? No way.

So that meant that whatever the American carried was no ordinary shotgun. The bullet spread went into the shisa's, mouth causing the head to explode into a thousand tiny pebbles that showered the room like an autumn rain over a thicket.

"Booyah," he said, mimicking my earlier victory dance.

"Funny," I said.

He cocked his gun again. "What was funny was your little maneuver after you'd just attacked the air."

Just as I was trying to think of something witty to say back, the closed-mouthed shisa jumped on the bar and then at the American. He let out two shots, but the guardian dog was too fast, tackling him to the ground.

"Deirdre, help him," I said as I tossed the longer of the two swords to Egya just in time for him to deflect a massive swing from Ungyo's own sword.

Agyo charged at me and I managed to roll out of the way as the diamond head of his vajra destroyed poor Kenji's tatami.

"I'll fix that!" I called out.

The bamboo mat split and before Agyo could swing again, I thrust my sword into its side.

Well, I tried to at least, but the damn Buddhist guardian was made of stone and my sword only managed to make an impressive *ping!* sound against his skin. So much for picking swords.

I barely managed to duck as he tried to elbow me. But I was lucky —I had anticipated his move. If he had swung his vajra or tried to kick me, he would have connected for sure. And there was no telling what a blow from something as powerful as this guy would do to me.

What's more, for stone statues, these things were fast. I mean, what kind of statue can move like that? I'd fought gargoyles before, and even the small ones couldn't move like this guy.

The Heralds kept chanting, and it occurred to me that if we knocked *them* out, these guardian statues—which were really more like the mystical equivalent of the Terminator … as in, just doing what they were programmed to do—might be easier to shut off. But every time I made a step toward the Heralds, a nio would stop my advance. Apparently protecting their animators was part of the programming.

We needed to get out of here.

I turned; Egya wasn't faring much better, spending all his energy just dodging the powerful swings of Ungyo's sword.

"Out the back," I said. "We need to—"

But my luck had run out. Agyo managed to give me a swift kick that sent me flying; I hit the wall with a thud and fell on my back. Agyo wasted no time running in my direction, seeking to finish me off with a single stomp of his foot.

I wonder what happens to someone who dies without a soul? I thought as the stone foot stamped down toward my head.

Except the sole of his carved sandal didn't make contact. Just as it was about to crush my cute button nose, I heard a shot and felt a shower of pebbles. I rolled away and saw Agyo fall to the ground, his left foot completely missing.

Another blast and the Agyo's head turned into dust.

"I'd say booyah again," the American said, "but I've got to help Ms. Marvel here with a stone dog problem." He turned and I saw Deirdre wrestling with the shisa. As strong as she was, I saw that it took every ounce of her strength to subdue the dog.

Then there was another blast and her struggle was over. I was starting to like this guy.

"A little help here," I said as I charged at Ungyo.

"On it," the American said, pumping his shotgun and pointing it at Ungyo's head. "Hasta la vista, baby," he said as he took off Ungyo's head.

The stone statue went down without so much as a whimper.

I straightened, brushing dust and golem bits off my clothes. "Thanks."

"Just doing my job, ma'am," he said.

"Terrible line."

"Nope," he said, shaking his head. "Not a line. Just the truth." And he pulled out a badge. "I'm with OAIU. Other Activities Investigative Unit, Division Special Forces."

So that was why he had a shotgun.

I stepped forward to read the name on the badge. "Jean-Luc Matthias?"

"Just Jean, pronounced John," he said. "My starship's in the shop."

He stuck out a hand. This time I was willing to take it, but before I could, the ground rumbled as six shisa and four more pairs of nio came crashing into the izakaya.

"OK Jean," I said, pronouncing it like *jeans*, "I don't suppose you have more shotguns?"

"No ma'am, I do not."

10

A TROUBLE OF GUARDIANS

*W*hat do you call a bunch of stone guardians hell-bent on killing you? A quarry? A masonry? A landslide? I'd have to figure out the technical term for this gang of super badass statues later—if there was a later. Given how these guys came at us, I wasn't so sure.

The two cloak-wearing weirdo humans pointed at us as they continued their odd chant. Three shisa advanced, and Jean let out two shots that reduced them to rubble. I didn't know how many bullets a shotgun could hold and started backing away from the izakaya's front door.

We needed to get out of there. Apparently Egya had already had that thought, because he yelled from the back room that there was a way out through the kitchen.

None of us needed to be told twice, and Jean let out two more shots, taking down a nio as the three of us followed Egya out the back door that led into the alley.

Now all we had to do was hope the guardians hadn't surrounded the place.

↔

No guardians in the back alley. Thank the GoneGods for small miracles.

What I wasn't thanking the GoneGods for was imbuing these guys with supernatural speed. We'd hardly made it outside by the time the shisa were on our backs, running along the walls of the alley rather than on the actual ground.

The nio guardians weren't far behind, their heavy feet like thunder as they chased after us. We were dead, dead, dead unless we escaped. Or were saved by a miracle.

Or both.

Just as we were approaching the end of the alley, a car pulled up, driven by a woman wearing a black scarf over her face that kind of gave her a ninja vibe (not to stereotype or anything, but we were in Japan). She screamed, *"Hayaku!"*

You didn't have to speak Japanese to understand what she was saying: *Hurry*.

↔

As we jumped into the back of her Honda Civic, I lamented that it wasn't something with a bit more kick. Then the woman floored the accelerator and I felt my body pushed against the back of the seat. Seems that in a godless world, my prayers were answered: this car had been modified.

It was fast.

But so were the shisa. Two of them managed to jump in front of the car before she could pick up much speed. Not that she slowed down; she kept that foot hot on the accelerator.

"Ahh," I said, "they're probably a couple tons of magically rein-forced stone. I don't think crashing into them is a good—"

The shishas were just about upon us when she pulled the hand-brake and screamed, "America-jin, to your left!"

Jean didn't need to be told twice. He cocked his shotgun and without bothering to open the window, blasted the two shisa with buckshot and glass. Both open-mouthed and closed-mouthed guardians went down in a hail of gravel and lead.

Damn, he was a good shot.

"I'm out," he said in that way only those with a lot of training say.

The driver hit the accelerator as she made a sharp turn. The path now clear, we started down the road until it dead-ended, then we turned left, then right, then left again.

Each turn slow us down, but we were still going fast enough that we were gaining ground on the shisa and nio. Two more turns and we'd be on the main highway, where we'd lose them for sure.

We turned left and I could see the main road just in front of us. One more turn and ... shit!

Two nio appeared at the T intersection. They must not have both-ered to pursue us, figuring we'd eventually make our way out of this back-road maze and end up right here.

Statues made of stone harder than diamond *and* clever. My luck was really on the wane today.

The young woman slammed her car into reverse and started backing up, but now four shisa and a pair of nio were behind us, too.

"Damn it," I said. "You're really out of bullets?"

Jean was looking behind him at the six approaching golems. "I'm afraid 'I'm out' isn't a euphemism for 'I've got more.' "

"And why don't you have more?"

"I had over twenty shells with me. On my night off ..."

I groaned. "Fine," I said, "we're just going to have to do this the hard way."

"And which way is that?"

"Deirdre, remember when we watched *Return of the Jedi* and you loved how the rebels took down those walkers?"

The changeling nodded.

"Good." I turned to the driver. "I saw a parking complex on the other side of Kokusai Dori. You know the one I'm talking about?"

The driver nodded.

"I'll meet you at the exit."

And before anyone could say anything, I opened the door and jumped out.

↔

Golems and guardians are the Terminators of the supernatural world. Which means they were programmed with a specific mission and weren't ones for improvisation. And since the guardians were after me—or more specifically, my arm that was attached to me—I figured they would only hurt those who got in the way of what they wanted.

As I ran across the road and into a small noodle shop, I had enough time to confirm that the guardians were all ignoring the Honda Civic and its occupants.

They just wanted me.

Sucks to be popular, I thought as I scanned the noodle house. It was empty save for the two cooks and a guy manning the register. *"Ikite!"* I cried out as I ran to the back.

The register guy barely had time to *register* what was happening when the nio came crashing through. *"Kowai,"* he screamed as he hugged the wall farthest from where I was.

Not that I stuck around to see what was happening. Instead, I ran through the back door and into another alley before slamming through another back door.

And with every place I ran into, the damn guardians crashed through, causing thousands of dollars of damage, ruining livelihoods and just generally being inconsiderate to those around them.

Soup bowls and chopsticks and tatami mats went flying. People screamed and ran. And the whole time, the statues didn't make a peep except to thunder through the buildings like bulls in, well—

Japanese shops. I had to say it, okay?

But they didn't hurt anyone. That privilege they were reserving for little old me.

I busted through the front door of a human-run izakaya and onto Kokusai Dori. The street was full of cars and people who were probably thinking that they were out for a meal and a bit of shopping. From the way they scattered when the nio and shisa jumped on the road, they certainly weren't expecting giant moving statues rampaging on the streets.

Still, the scattering crowds provided some cover and as long as the guys didn't have some kind of homing beacon or mythical-map-finding app, I could use them as cover.

I ran inside another building, this one attached to the parking complex, and paused against a pillar to catch my breath. There was no way they could have tracked my movement in that crowd, so I was safe. At least, that was my hope. Peering out the window, I saw several nio looking back and forth down the road.

Good—no mythical tracking device.

Then the nio—Ungyo—looked right at me. And it wasn't like he was looking around and happened to see me. No, he stopped looking back and forth and stared right at me like he knew exactly where I was the whole time.

What the hell? I thought, not waiting for the guy to jump through the window. I heard the crash of stone and glass as I made my way to the back of the building and toward the parking lot. I needed to get to the complex's entrance, where hopefully my friends would be waiting for me and—

I felt a granite hand grab my shoulder and push me to the side, sending my body flying until it hit the wall.

I had just enough breath to climb to my feet and see two nio guardians approaching me, Agyo holding his diamond mace before him and that forever-open mouth promising nothing good.

Oh joy.

. . .

↔

So this was how it would end? Being bludgeoned to death by a stone golem with an attitude? And to think, they'd go to all this trouble to kill me and I didn't even know where the place they were guarding actually *was*. I mean, you'd think that they'd have extended the courtesy of at least letting me find the place before killing me.

Not that any of that mattered. I was out of breath, out of strength and out of luck. All I had time for now was to consider whether or not to keep my eyes open or closed while they beat me into the linoleum floor, ruining some poor janitor's day.

"Open," I muttered to myself. "I will face my death with eyes open."

I scowled at Agyo and Ungyo as they approached, using the wall as support to shuffle myself up to my feet. "So," I said, "what's it like being a mythical guardian?"

Neither Agyo nor Ungyo's expressions changed, the demon-like faces frozen open and closed. They were only a couple steps away, spreading out just enough so that if I tried to run to the left or right, they could easily catch me.

I'd chased down enough victims as a vampire to know when running was pointless. I wasn't going to run.

And I wasn't going to beg or cry or quiver in fear. I was going to meet my end as best I could.

Weaponless, I gave them the finger. When they didn't react to that, I dug into my pockets and pulled out some loose change and threw it at them. I knew it would have no effect, but if I was going to die, I was going to die fighting ... as pointless as that fighting may be.

I dug deeper into my pockets looking for a quarter or, if I was lucky, a twoonie to throw at them, but I was out of change. All I had left in my pocket was that stupid shell with the rune etched into it.

The one that the futakuchi-onna left behind when I'd "stabbed" her with her own, invisible spear.

"Beggars can't be choosers," I said and took careful aim, hitting Agyo right in his stupid open mouth as he lifted his vajra. "Come on!" I screamed. "Make it clean. Right here." I pointed a finger at my forehead.

But the Agyo didn't bring his vajra down on my head. Instead he waved his hand like he was chasing away an invisible bee.

I looked over at Ungyo, who was doing the same. First with one hand, then both, until they were both dancing in that way someone would do when consumed by a swarm of bees.

There were no bees to speak of. There was nothing there. That didn't stop the awkward dancing from growing more and more frantic. Whatever it was, I wasn't going to look a gift horse (or an invisible swarm) in the mouth. I charged to the left and toward the entrance of the parking complex.

Before I could get into the parking lot, I saw what looked like three children watching me run, their expressionless faces sad and distant.

Three children who didn't run when two giant golems showed up.

Three children who were probably dead.

I looked at them, then back at the nio guardians. They continued their dance, but where I hadn't seen anything before, now I saw the statues surrounded by hundreds of mokumokuren, the floating eyeballs annoying them like any bee or wasp would when defending their hive.

"What the—?" I started, then remembered the ghost kids. "I really should mind my language. Sorry."

↔

After that, I managed to get to the entrance without encountering any more guardians. The driver and my friends were waiting for me. So was the American, Jean. I had hoped he'd break away when the heat was off him, but he was still sitting there, grinning away.

Deirdre was waiting outside the car, the passenger side door open. "Milady," she said as I jumped in.

"Where are the golems?" Egya asked.

"Dealing with a swam of eyeballs," I said, happy to be sitting.

"What?"

"Later," I said, closing my eyes. "Just give me a few minutes to catch my breath."

And that's what I got. A few minutes while our savior drove toward the shore about thirty minutes away.

↔

"So, not that I'm not grateful, but who are you?" I said.

The woman took a sharp turn over the road's divide before turning into an alley barely wide enough for the car. Boy oh boy, this lady could drive. "Tomoko-san told me that the great Katrina Darling had arrived. I had to see it for myself. Of course, the guardians arrived before me and—"

"Tomoko-san?"

"Yes, the hostess at the izakaya. The onryo."

So that was why she'd scurried past us so quickly. She needed to tell this lady, whoever she was, that we were here. I really needed to work on my incognito skills.

I took another couple deep breaths before turning to my savior and taking a good look at her for the first time. For her shape and size, I judged her to be a young woman in her early twenties. She had long black hair and big brown, captivating eyes.

"Thank you," I said.

"No," she said, removing her scarf, "it is I who should thank you."

When I saw her face, my heart jumped in a way that I had only ever felt once before. *How could this be?* I wondered as I reached out a hand to touch her face. *How could she be so young?*

My voice trembled as I called out her name. "Blue?"

11

REUNIONS AND SOUL-BEATING MOMENTS

"Y ou honor me," the girl said with a refined English accent, like she had been tutored by Alfred or someone equally posh, "but I am not Blue. She is my grandmother, but the gods have blessed me with her strong appearance."

"Grandmother?"

She nodded before bowing deeply, an awkward move given that she was still sitting on the driver's side of the car. "I am Keiko Uehara and I offer you my gratitude for saving my grandmother, thus allowing me to be brought into this world."

"Ahh, grandmother," Jean said. "Which means that you, not-so-young lady, are not human. Or maybe you're one of those now-I'm-supernatural, now-I'm-not types. So what were you? A werewolf? Vampire? Zombie?"

"Milady is no foul, flesh-eating zombie," Deirdre said, jumping to my defense.

"Well, excuse me," Jean said, lathering his words with sarcasm.

Sarcasm was always lost on Deirdre. "You are excused. This once," she said very seriously.

"So which one were you?"

"There's more than just werewolves and vampires," Egya said, then sticking out a hand, added, "Former were-hyena."

"Were-hyena? I didn't know weres came in hyena size."

"Actually, there are all kinds of weres."

"Apparently." Jean lifted a hand. "Nice to meet you, Hyena."

"It's Egya."

"Is that African for 'hyena?' "

"No, and that's mildly racist."

"Not if Egya actually meant hyena," Jean said, not missing a beat. "So milady, you were pretty handy with a sword back there, which means that you're quite comfortable fighting in human form. So I'm going to go with vampire."

"The American wins the prize," Egya said, still a bit sore about the hyena jibe.

I ignored him, just as I had been ignoring the whole conversation. I just stared at Keiko, imagining that this was how Blue must have looked as a young woman. Then that got me thinking about how she must have looked as a teenager, middle-aged, pregnant. Holy guacamole, Blue was a grandmother, which meant she was a mother and ...

"I missed it all," I said. And trying as I hard as I did, I still couldn't hold back the tears that had threatened to escape since I'd seen this young woman's face.

"No, you just weren't here for it all. But you were with us. Always." She understood what I was feeling. And in order to do that, her empathy had to be enormous.

Just like Blue's.

↔

I gave Keiko a hug which turned into an embrace that probably lasted longer than what was socially acceptable for two people who'd just met—at least in Canadian, Scottish and Japanese culture.

Apparently it was a bit too much for American culture, too, because Jean said, "Alright, ladies. Not to break up what I'm sure Egya and I are hoping will turn into kissing, but angry stone guardians. Somewhere behind us. Got to get somewhere safe."

Damn it, I thought. *As much as I hate to admit it, this annoying American is right.*

"I'll have you know that a lot of people find me charming," he said.

Thinking out loud again. I shook my head and finally let go of Keiko. "Thank you for saving us. As you can see, we're in a wee bit of trouble, so if you could drop us off at our hotel and the American at wherever Americans go, we'll be—"

"No way," Jean and Keiko said in unison.

"Excuse me?"

Jean was the first to speak, lifting his butt up enough to dig his wallet out of his back pocket. He tossed it to me and I opened it up, seeing his badge. "I can't let you go, ma'am," he said, his voice getting all authoritative. "You were attacked by several class-B and -C Others. Until we know what's going on, I can't permit you to leave. I'll have to take you to base to continue our ongoing investigation."

Ongoing investigation my ass, I thought.

Before I could answer, Keiko piped in, "We have been waiting for years for your return, Katto-san. My grandmother will kill me if I do not bring you to her. In addition, I owe you a blood debt. I shall aid you until we know that you are safe."

"First of all," I said, pointing at Jean, "I'm not under your jurisdiction, so you can shove your investigation into the orifice near where you got this." I tossed his badge back to him.

"I'm afraid I can't accept that," he said.

"Do you have magical powers?" I asked.

"Excuse me?"

"I said, 'do you have magical powers?' "

"Not that I'm aware of."

"Good, because that's the only way you'll be able to take us in. Not unless you plan on fighting an ex-vampire, ex-were-hyena, a changeling and a ninja."

By which I meant Keiko, who I had no doubt—given her driving skills and her heritage—could lay some smack down.

"I see your point," he said with a resigned grin.

"And as for you, young lady, I want nothing more than to see Blue again. Believe me. But I cannot risk endangering her. Or you, for that matter. You saw those things. They'd destroy her home and—"

"I have been training my whole life for a chance to protect you, Katto-san." Keiko lifted her sword before me. "I am ready to help. And once we have restored peace to your life, then we will go to my grand-mother. Agreed?"

Her eyes met mine and I saw the same stubborn, fearless determi-nation I had seen in Blue all those years ago. There wasn't a force in this world or any other that would deter her from her mission. She would help me get those damned golems off my back and then she would bring me to meet her grandmother.

And I was going to let her.

"OK," I said, nodding.

"OK," she repeated, a wide, Cheshire Cat grin painted her face.

"So," I said, turning to everyone in the backseat except Jean, "after we get rid of this guy, what's our next move?"

And that's when I saw the beeping light in Jean's shirt pocket. "What's that?"

"This?" he said, fishing out the little device. "I was thinking about what you said—about what I'd need to take you in and all. And well, while I don't have magical powers, I do have—"

We heard the loud whoosh of helicopter blades as a Warbird landed not twenty feet from where we were parked.

"—that," he said.

12

MA'AMS, METAL TABLES AND SOLE EYEBALLS

A significant part of Okinawa is covered with U.S. military bases. It was one of the conditions settled upon at the end of World War II, and although this is a sour point for the local population, their presence is mostly peaceful. Mostly.

Every now and then, some U.S. marine or army personnel does something culturally inappropriate or horrific or illegal, or all three. The locals protest, arrests are made and things return to an uneasy peace. All that said, in the years since the war, there were very few instances of violence on any large scale. Still, resentment against the bases exists. Understandable, really ... would you want a foreign army in your backyard?

As the decades rolled on after the war, things had been peaceful enough that there had been significant talks about moving the bases from mainland Okinawa to the outer islands or even mainland Japan. Agreements had been drafted, plans were made, but as advanced as those talks had been, when the gods left, the U.S. military backpedaled on the deal. The world had changed in unimaginable ways and they didn't want to lose their Asian presence in case Earth's new citizens tried to, you know ... take over the world, starting with Japan.

If anything, the arrival of the Others increased the presence of U.S. military on the island.

Just another side-effect of the gods leaving.

Sure, the Others' presence was something that made everyone nervous, but again, any fighting between humans and Others tended to be isolated incidents, not full-scale attacks. Things had been pretty tame.

Or so I'd thought.

Given everything I thought I knew, I figured we'd fly into your typical peacetime army base. But as the chopper flew us onto Kadena Air Base, I didn't see a peacetime base.

What I saw was a place gearing up for war.

Soldiers were doing drills by the hundreds as grunts moved enough supplies and equipment to arm an—well, an army. And I knew just by the sheer, staggering numbers: of people, of gear, of supplies.

They had enough stockpiled here to outlast a dozen apocalypses. But that wasn't the most stunning part.

There was equipment with the classic Memnock Securities logo on it, three rings that overlapped to form a triangle of circles:

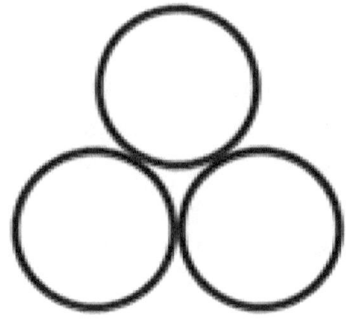

That logo struck fear in every Other that saw it, and from the way Deirdre and Egya drew in their breaths, I knew they'd encountered equipment by those guys before, too.

They were the arms dealers that specialized in anti-Other weaponry. Finely tuned clocks with radar functionality that could detect magic being burned from miles away. Electrified, steel-wire nets specially designed to make angel and valkyrie wings useless. Custom-made grenades filled with all kinds of stuff Others were allergic to: wood splinters for dwarves, holy water for demons, toad tongues for goblins, cat hairs for pixies. Fish hook-style missile harpoons with heat-seeking guidance systems for dragons. The list went on and on, with all kinds of nasties specifically designed to capture, maim or kill Others.

There were crates and crates of this stuff being unloaded from ships at the harbor. The only reason you'd stockpile so much equipment was if you were preparing for war.

Not good, I thought.

"Well," Jean said, eavesdropping on my thoughts, "that depends on who's side you're on."

↔

Egya, Deirdre and I were to be separated before being escorted to our individual holding cells. But before they could pry us apart, I ran over and hugged Egya like he was the love of my life and I couldn't stand to be away from him.

Jean, whom I pegged to have a wee bit of a romantic streak in him, let us embrace and as we did, I used some slight-of-hand tricks I'd learned over the centuries to get the Soul Amulet into Egya's pocket. I knew what was coming and the last thing I wanted was some military geek figuring out the amulet was magical ... and I figured that since the nio were after me, they wouldn't look at Egya quite as closely as me.

↔

I wanted to wring Jean's neck, but given that they showed their hospitality by handcuffing us, I settled on giving him a look of death.

"If looks could kill ..." he said, guiding me to a holding room. "And you're welcome."

"For what? Handcuffing us? Locking us up?"

"For saving your ass back at the izakaya."

"Hardly. We had it under control."

"Sure you did," he said, giving me a wide grin before closing the door and leaving me alone in the cell.

I sat down on the one chair provided, placing my shackled hands on the cool metal table. The walls had soundproofed paneling, two cameras tucked away in the upper corners of the room and a two-way mirror. I'd like to say that these circumstances weren't familiar to me, but that would be a bold-faced lie.

This was the second time I'd been inside one of these rooms this year (I'd snuck one in just before the New Year ... yay me!).

Perhaps my New Year's resolution should have been to avoid these places, but then again, perhaps not. I liked giving myself goals that were doable, like eating healthier or not getting killed.

Or retrieving a missing soul.

So I did what I always do when waiting to be interrogated. I sat perfectly still, replaying my favorite movie in my head: *Legally Blonde*.

I was at the part where Reese had just gotten into Harvard when the door opened. It was Jean, standing there with a backpack and an I-got-you grin. "OK," he said, "you were definitely a vampire. Ex-vamps are the only kind of humans that can sit perfectly still like that." He seemed unsurprised.

"So in your world, excellent meditation skills means ex-vamp? I hardly think my zen-ness warrants such an accusation."

"Yeah, maybe. But then again, we have this," he said, putting a file down on the table. "You haven't registered."

"Was I meant to?"

"Says here that you're a normal girl. You did a good job covering your tracks and if I hadn't seen you do what you did, I might have actually believed that you are a normal human girl. But normal human girls don't dress like this."

He dropped a photo of me in my cherub mask and dirk and kilt that was my clan's pattern. Granted, women didn't wear kilts back when I was a teenager, but times change, and why should the men have all the fun?

I looked at the pictures. They were from when I'd fought a bunch of wannabe superheroes on campus about twenty-four hours before I was turned into a vampire (for the second time) and lost my soul (also for the second time).

"Why do you think that's—?"

"You, and not some other Scottish girl with extraordinary fighting abilities? Oh, I don't know … detective work." Then he showed me another photo of me stuffing my costume into the vent in a McGill arts building bathroom. "Welcome to this brave new GoneGod world. There are cameras everywhere."

He picked up one of the zoomed-in photos and touched my masked face. "What are you supposed to be, anyway? A fighting baby? Is your superpower throwing tantrums?"

"Oh, haha," I said, seeing no sense in denying it. "I'm part of the Divine Order of Cherub Hunters. An organization my father—"

"—started a few months after you were turned. Right around the time you turned your mother and about three years before you turned your father," he said, reading from a file. "We know."

"How?" The fact that I'd turned my mother was common knowledge, but me turning my father … that was something only I (and Mergen) knew. And Mergen, being an avatar of truth, was incapable of telling others my secrets.

So it was really the same as if only I knew.

"We didn't," he said. "Just a guess. You father went missing three years later and I put one and one together. Detective work, Ms. Darling." The kariyushi-wearing soldier tapped the bulb he called a head.

Totally underestimated you, I thought. *You're not nearly as stupid as your shirt.*

"Again, kariyushi-wear is the thing here," he said, apparently listening in on my thoughts. "Anyway, all of that is to say, we might not have taken as close a look at you had you not been at the izakaya meeting with one of the biggest Yakuza leaders in town."

This caught my interest. "Kenji is part of the mob?"

"An Other boss." Jean waved a dismissive hand, then returning to an earlier conversation, pointed at a photo of Cherub-me. "You know, the amnesty program is a must. It's the only way to be forgiven for all the people you, you know ..." He made a sucking sound.

"I don't need your forgiveness," I growled. "Not when I'll never forgive myself."

Jean narrowed his eyes like he was examining a puzzle and not little ol' me. "That may be," he finally said, "but the amnesty program is the only way to expunge your past. Look here, Ms. Darling, we're willing to give you a clean slate. All you have to do is register."

"So that when some asshole gets elected and policies change, we're all the easier to hunt down," I said.

Jean pursed his lips, but didn't disagree with me. He seemed to understand where I was coming from and had been around the block enough times to know I had a point.

"OK, we'll circle back to this later. For now, I have this one burning question. Why were souped-up, supernatural guardian golems after someone as cute as a button?"

"You hitting on me, soldier?"

"No," he said honestly. That, or he was one hell of an actor. "It's just that young girls like you tend to be into partying, dancing, school. You know, typical stuff that—"

"—humans do," I said. "Believe me, I'm trying." I shook my head.

"But how do you know they were after me and not, I don't know, trying to take out a human spy?"

He gave me a look that said, *"Come on."*

I shrugged. "See, not as stupid as you look. Fine, they *were* after me, but I have no idea—"

He started with that look again, but before he could fully form his condescending face, I added, "I don't. I swear."

"You're going to have to give me something. If, that is, you want out of here. As in, ever."

I didn't know what to say. I couldn't tell him about my soul or the Soul Jar, so I just sat quietly and waited to see how this whole thing would play out.

That's when the two of us commenced a stare-off the last for about ten minutes before he finally broke it with an eye-roll and a, "OK … you win. But not really …"

He pulled a laptop from his backpack and a little USB with a mic at one side. He plugged it and I heard my voice play back, followed by Kenji's.

"You bugged me?" I said.

"Shush," he said, "I haven't listened to this yet. I thought we could listen to it together."

I pursed my lips as the conversation between Kenji and me played in the interrogation room. I heard myself talk about the map and futakuchi-onna ghost. A rustling sounded when I tried to show the nurikabe my invisible map.

Then Kenji said the magic words: Kami Subete Hakubutsukan.

Once those words were uttered, my Big Trouble status got upgraded to Disastrous.

↔

The door burst in and an aigamuchab wearing army fatigues walked into the room. The faceless creature put her flat, eyeless surface right in front of my face and started clicking … their way of seeing.

I knew what this creature was, although I'd never seen one myself. They were legendary as vicious hunters with incredible speed and strength. And despite not having a face (and the eyes that tended to go with faces), they had built-in radar. A few well-timed clicks and they could see better than most eye-card-holding creatures. Other than the whole facelessness and incessant clicking, they looked like humans, and this one had a gymnast's physique locked in a six-foot frame.

She clicked three more times before saying, "Kami Subete Hakubutsukan? You possess a map to Kami Subete Hakubutsukan?" Her voice sounded like shattering glass.

"First of all, you're in my personal space. Secondly, it was only a theory. I have no idea where this map leads to."

The aigamuchab clicked twice more before saying, "A treasure hunter?"

"Possibly, General Shouf," Jean said.

"General?" I said, "Really? You're a general for a human army."

"Yes," Shouf shattered, "I am."

"Humph," I said, appraising the general. The OAIU was known to kill first and be reasonable second. They were ruthless and vicious, taking down Others for minor offenses. Brutally efficient, too.

And it seemed some of that efficiency came from their Other general. I would have branded her a traitor, but who was to say that different kinds of mythical creatures had to be loyal to anyone but their own?

Common decency, I supposed.

But then again, such principles were in short supply these days.

"The map—where is it?" Shouf asked.

There was no point hiding it. I pulled back my sleeve and showed them my arm, where *I* saw swirling mists of blue and orange and red outlining Okinawa's shoreline.

But of course, only I could see it. Jean took a closer look. "Oh, haha. There's nothing there."

"For you. For me, I see … well, I see a map."

"She's messing with us."

General Shouf clicked twice before saying, "I don't know, Jean-Luc." The human soldier cringed at his full name being used. "She may not be. Tell me, young vampire, how is it that you came into possession of the map?"

I didn't want to tell her about the amulet sitting in Egya's pocket—or losing my soul to some messed up curse. Nor that I was in touch with some strange stalker guy who could give her a run for the creepiest voice ever. So instead I pulled a line used by dozens of tough-guy heroes in hundreds of books and movies. "I know a guy."

"I'm sure you do," the aigamuchab said.

Jean lifted his arms in exasperation. "See? Messing with us."

The general shook her head. "You judge too quickly. Yes, she is not telling us what we seek to know, but that doesn't mean there is no truth in her obfuscation. It is legend that those who seek the Kami Subete Hakubutsukan must have a legitimate claim to an item that resides within its divine halls. *A legitimate claim,*" General Shouf repeated, slowly emphasizing each word. "Only then will the location be revealed, and even then, only to the bearer of said claim."

The aigamuchab walked over to the other side of the table and motioned for Jean to stand up. "Do you mind?"

"Certainly, ma'am," Jean said, standing.

General Shouf sat down and slowly removed her boots as she continued shattering words at us. "The things those halls hold are so magnificent that even the gods could not contain their power. The only way to hold the power *in* was by giving them an outlet to seep *out* into this world. A one-way conduit, constantly releasing the pressure of the powder keg held within."

The aigamuchab lifted her feet onto the table so that the soles of her feet faced me. Her heels stirred as two eyes opened and stared directly at me.

Or rather, *in* me.

↔

"That is hella creepy," I said.

Jean nodded in agreement. "I'll never get used to it."

General Shouf ignored us both as the eyes continued looking at me, narrowing in deep contemplation as she scoured every inch of me in one of the most violating experiences I've ever had.

I wasn't just being closely looked at—I was being examined while power exuded out of those horrible eyes. I could feel that they weren't looking through me, but *in* me, and to have such a foreign presence exploring my insides was horrible.

"Will you … will you stop it, please?" I said, starting to lose control over myself. I hadn't wanted to give them the satisfaction of showing discomfort or pain, but this was getting to be too much. "Please," I repeated, unable to hide the panic in my voice.

She ignored me, her horrific eyes continuing to scan me.

"Stop it, stop it, stop it!" I yelled.

Still nothing.

I tried to stand up, but Jean quickly got behind me and forced me back into my seat with two strong hands. I struggled against them, but couldn't move. He was strong. Very strong.

"Let me go," I growled.

Still the eyes performed their violation. And just when I thought I couldn't take it anymore, the eyelids closed and Shouf took her feet off the table.

"I see now," she said. "Your soul. That is your claim."

With that she stood up and walked out of the room, leaving her shoes behind. "Jean-Luc—if you will," she said from the hall.

Jean let go of my shoulders and started for the door. He paused at the threshold and turned to me.

I didn't look up at him, still reeling from those horrible eyes and what they'd done to me. I wanted to run, to scream, but I knew there was nothing I could do but sit there and breathe.

I took several deep breaths before I heard Jean leave the room and close the door behind him.

13

A MILLION SCREENS AND
EYELESS CREEPS

I had just enough time to center myself again before the door flew open and a red-faced Jean stomped in. Whatever discussion had happened outside, it hadn't pleased him. Nor had it taken long. He threw me a set of keys and made a *hurry up* gesture.

As I freed myself from my shackles, he gestured for me to follow. I thought about resisting, being difficult, refusing to leave, putting the cuffs back on—you know, just to show him who was boss. But the thought that I was actually being set free compelled me to cooperate. If I was really lucky, Deirdre, Egya and I would be back at our hotel before dawn.

But luck hadn't been with me on this trip.

As I followed Jean through the base, passing by theater rooms with dozens of eggheads writing on clear boards, computers beeping and booping and radars pinging, I realized that getting out of this place was the last thing on their minds.

We entered a room with dozens of screens showing different parts of the base. On them, I saw the full extent of this base and the preparations they were undertaking. It wasn't just equipment being stockpiled, but equipment being unpacked for use. As in, use *right now*. The way the soldiers were gearing up, they were preparing for deployment to only the GoneGods knew where.

But it was New Year's. If anything, the base should have been operating with a skeleton crew while the majority of the troops went off to party. Especially given the time of year and that there wasn't any major fighting going on anywhere that required such force. If there was, the news would have been all over it and the world would be at DEFCON 1 or 5—whatever passed as the highest state of alert.

I also noted several digital clocks on the wall with the names of locations printed over them: Paris, New York, Hong Kong, Melbourne … Montreal. These clocks weren't of the time-telling variety, though; they were used to monitor any major magical activities, and from the progression of time, very little magic was being used in those areas. But these clocks weren't limited to major cities. Other, smaller towns and hamlets were being monitored, too. Scotland's Inverness, Egypt's Fayoum, Canada's Cardiff, New Zealand's Hobbit Town, Cotswold, Strun, Paradise Lot and dozens of other places I'd never heard of.

None of them were counting down to New Year's (which was only an hour away), but rather, didn't seem to tell time at all. There was a master clock that hung above the screens which was counting the exact years, months, weeks, days, hours, minutes and seconds since the gods left. None of the other clocks were in sync with the master clock because the other clocks were measuring magic use. Every time magic was used in one of those locations, the clock would speed up just a bit, providing an accurate measurement of how much magic was used and where.

Also, the location choices of these clocks were immediately apparent: they were all places that had a reasonably high Other presence. With the exception of Paradise Lot, an unofficial Other sanctuary, none of the clocks had sped up too much, being out of sync with the master clock by a few weeks at most. And even in Paradise Lot, it seemed the use of magic was very limited, with only a year of additional time spent.

So where the hell were these troops going?

↔

Despite the room being filled with screens and computers and other pieces of equipment that would be any gadget-addicted geek's wet dream, there was no one else here.

Well, no one if you didn't include Jean, General Shouf and me. Seeing the aigamuchab again made my heart cringe. "You're not going to *sole* gaze me again," I said, pointing at her feet.

She didn't react. Neither did Jean.

"You know, sole. As in the *sole* of your foot, but it sounds like 'soul,' as in life force, spirit—"

"We get it," Jean said.

"Chi," I muttered.

"Ha-ha," Jean said, pulling out a chair for me to sit.

I sat. Huffily, I might add.

"Ms. Darling," the aigamuchab crackled, "I believe we have gotten off to a poor start. I want to offer you my humblest apologizes for my little intrusion earlier."

"Intrusion? An interesting word for what you did to me. I'd go more for mental rape." And I meant that word in all the ugliness it implied. I'd never felt more violated or powerless before—and if the GoneGods willed it, I would never feel that way again.

Jean cringed at the word.

General Shouf only nodded. "You are not the first to put it that way and I am sure you will not be the last. If it makes you feel better, know that I burned almost two weeks of time to examine you."

"Given a convicted rapist gets ten years plus ... no, no it doesn't make me feel better."

"I understand," General Shouf said. "But do allow me to put into context why I went to such extreme lengths to extract the information that you were so unwilling to provide."

Before I could think of a snarky reply, she pushed a button and the disconnected base security monitors unified into one large, theater screen that showed a video of the night the gods left.

What I saw were the typical scenes that had been played a million times on the news and in documentaries about the GrandExodus: the sky turning blood red as angels fell like comets, volcanos erupting with dragons, frog creatures and mermaids and kelpie swirling at the shores, dwarves pouring out of the gold mines of Papua New Guinea.

I yawned at the miraculous scene of the divine being poured onto Earth. "Yeah, seen it all before. Your point?"

General Shouf didn't shift, instead waiting patiently as the screens displayed the first weeks of the Others' arrival. Attacks, fights, anger, protesting. The world in chaos. Again, all familiar stuff.

Until it wasn't. The screens shifted to a zoomed-out display of what must have been a hundred battleships all focusing their cannon fire in the sky. Their bombardment was accompanied by several fighter jets and Apache Warbirds also concentrating their fire ... on what?

Despite the size of the screen, I had to stand up to get a closer look before I understood what they were firing at. In the center of that concentrated arsenal was a single angel darting around the screen like a hummingbird moving from flower to flower.

Except those puffs of smoke weren't flowers. They were bombs exploding midair as they tried to kill a lone angel. At one point the angel dove into the water, his body crashing through a hull and sinking a battleship. He emerged from the water, grabbing an Apache Warbird and removing its propellers as if plucking petals from a blossom.

"When was this?" I asked, still staring at the screen.

"November 20th," General Shouf said.

Three days after I'd lost my soul.

On screen, the battle went on for a long while, the angel dismantling this Armageddon piece by piece, all the while taking heavy fire himself. I could see that he was being hurt. I could also see him aging as he burned time, using his magic to put up one hell of a fight.

The screen went blank. "That was the archangel Gabriel," General

Shouf's voice crackled, "and he took down four more battleships before we finally managed to stop him."

"You mean kill him," I said, turning to look at the faceless aigamuchab.

The general shrugged. "In the end we lost nearly a billion dollars of equipment in just one battle. A battle, might I add, that we nearly lost."

"Interesting that you put the loss in terms of dollars and not bodies," I said.

General Shouf shrugged, but I could see from how Jean looked away that he was clearly pissed off about that, too. As a soldier, he thought in terms of people, his brothers and sisters in arms, and not dollars. Clearly, that was something he and his eyeless general didn't agree on.

"Dollars—bodies," the general continued. "The point is, one Other did all that. Granted, the archangel Gabriel was a particularly powerful Other, but still."

"He wanted to die," Jean murmured. "Being Christian, he wanted to commit suicide. He picked a fight with us in the hope that we would end him. He could have flown away—he could have done so many other things besides fight to the end."

"Why?" I said.

Jean shrugged. It was clear neither of them knew.

The general stood up, clicking twice to orientate herself in the room, and walked over to me. "Humans do not have magic to defend themselves. You, more than most, must understand that. After all, you once had access to unlimited power, and now ..."

She let her words trail off. She was right, of course. As a vampire, I was impossibly strong, fast and had heightened senses that were an asset in just about any situation. And those were just some of my natural abilities. But now that I was human ... well, my fragility was made abundantly clear as I tried to move about, my muscles sore from fighting the nio and shisa guardians, my body aching from all the times they hit me or threw me against a wall.

They hurt me in ways that wouldn't have even registered as a vampire. And the memory of what my strength was before only accentuated my weaknesses now.

I nodded, not that the blind aigamuchab saw that.

"I know that you are no fool. No vampire as old as you could be," Shouf said. Then she took on a casual tone, as if we were at some cocktail party. "Did you know that less than two percent of all vampires are alive today? That is a fact most are unaware of, vampires included."

I shook my head; I hadn't known any vampires in my earlier years. My own sire had disappeared before we got a chance to "get to know each other"—whatever that would have entailed. When I started to meet other vamps, well, that was a statistic they never shared. No surprise there—vampires aren't really the numbers or the sharing type.

"Indeed. One of the questions on the registry is, 'How many vampires have you sired?' Based on the answers and allowing for error, lies, exaggerations and vampires who have yet to register"—she pointed at me—"our calculations put survival rates at under two percent. Correlate that with legend, lore, record-keeping and so on, and we further estimate that the average vampire survives less than ten years. There are several reasons for this: underestimating their own strength, failing to properly time sunrises, gorging on heavily fortified locals. Again, the list goes on, but all those reason can be boiled down to one overarching theme: stupidity."

General Shouf put a hand on my shoulder. I pulled away, swatting her claw-like hand like I was avoiding a scorpion. Again, she shrugged. "Stupidity," she repeated. "When you have almost unlimited power you tend to think nothing can kill you, so you get stupid. But *you* never got stupid, did you? Three hundred years and not only are you still alive, but there is virtually no record of you or your escapades. You must be a very clever, careful girl."

"Not that clever," I said, "given where I am now."

"Don't be so hard on yourself. It was a case of bad luck. We weren't looking for you—we were monitoring Kenji's activities, gathering intel on all this." She clicked another button and the scene of the soldiers preparing outside returned.

"Yeah," I said, "I was meaning to ask you about that. I mean, that's a lot of kids who aren't getting time off on New Year's. Overtime alone must be killing your budget."

If General Shouf caught my facetiousness, she made no indication of it. She simply nodded. "Indeed, but they knew what they signed up for, and evil takes no holidays."

I groaned. "Clichés aside, can you get to the point? I know that you're trying to recruit me, otherwise you wouldn't have uncuffed me and been so apologetic—by the way, apology still not accepted—or brought me to your little fishbowl. So I know you want me to work for you, and I'm guessing it has to do with the map only I can see. But knowing all that, I still don't know why."

The aigamuchab smiled. "Like I said: clever girl."

14

CARROTS, STICKS & THE REALIZATION

THAT MUSEUMS AREN'T JUST FOR TOURISTS

"We're under attack," General Shouf said.

"As in, now?" I asked with a huge dollop of sarcasm.

"Not at this moment, Ms. Darling, but soon," the general said gravely. I really had to stop using sarcasm with Others.

General Shouf pushed a button, bringing into focus a camera that showed a scene somewhere off the shore of the base. She clicked another two buttons and the camera zoomed in without image quality loss. Another click and the camera turned to night vision, showing something —or rather, some*things*—skidding along the surface of the water.

"Are those ... mermaids?" I asked.

"Mermaids and mermen—meres," Jean said, putting his feet up on the table. "We detected their advancement off the shore of Taiwan about twelve hours ago. At their current speed, they should be here by morning."

"Here? As in *here*, here?" I said.

"Yep," Jean said.

"You don't seem too disturbed by the prospect of being attacked by a—a ... what do you call a bunch of meres? A school?"

Jean chuckled at this. "We'll be ready."

"Indeed," shattered General Shouf. "There is no error in the timing of their attack. They were hoping that we would be celebrating the human new year. Given the past attacks—"

"Sorry, did you say past attacks? As in plural?"

"They've been attacking human military facilities with increasing regularity for the last six months," Jean said.

"No way," I said reverting to my 70's vernacular as I registered my own surprise. "There was nothing on the news and—"

"Ma'am, we're the military, not public schooling. The media knows what we tell them and we don't tell them much. Besides, up until now all attacks have been against military facilities. The Others are organizing themselves and, as I mentioned earlier, they have yet to mess with any civilian areas. We believe that they're probing us, searching for weaknesses."

"Probing? Really? They're mythical creatures, not aliens. They don't 'probe.' When they fight, they fight for glory or honor or whatever meres hold dear. They look for victory or a glorious death worthy of being recorded in the annals of legend. They're not really the let's-find-the-humans'-weaknesses type."

"Indeed," agreed General Shouf.

Jean nodded. "You're right, of course, but those were mythical, divine, gonna-live-forever Others. These guys are different, more organized than we thought. More vicious and—"

"They have a leader," I said, the implications hitting me for the first time. The reason why there was never an Other uprising or heavy attacks was because they were always disconnected. Different pantheons didn't play well with other Others, often holding grudges thousands of years old.

But if someone could unite them ... well, then it would be a different ball game all together. A raging minotaur could cause a lot of damage, but *one* was still manageable. A stampede of minotaurs all stomping their way toward a common goal, now that was a different story.

"Clever girl," General Shouf repeated. It was really starting to tick me off, probably like it ticked off the velociraptors in *Jurassic Park.*

And when velociraptors get ticked off, they eat you.

"Hey, Windshield for a Forehead. Call me 'clever girl' again and I'm going to show you just how stupid I can be." I took two loud steps in her direction just so she could *hear* my posturing.

She clicked, then nodded. "My apologies," she said, and I noted that when I threatened his superior officer, the grunt didn't even move. If anything, he smiled as if he wanted to see me deck this asshole of a general.

General Shouf clicked twice more before saying, "They have a leader." She called up a photo of an average looking angel ... and, of course, when I say average looking, I mean he was drop dead, I just want to die in your arms, gorgeous. Tall with a muscular build, lush blond hair, a chiseled chin and lips that wouldn't just kiss you ... they'd ignite you. Just as I was getting all googly eyed, the picture disappeared and with a shattering click from General Shouf, reality came rushing back in.

"Who?" I asked.

"It was Gabriel—"

I pointed at the screen where the angel had been.

Jean shook his head. "No, that's not Gabriel ... the archangel is gone. Dead. That image is of their new leader; a lesser angel that goes by the name Daniel."

Jean stopped talking and I made a go on gesture.

The soldier shrugged.

"I'm afraid that's about all we know. A name, a picture and a vague idea of their mission. We also know that more and more Others have been gathering in Okinawa. Why?" General Shouf said, asking the question on my lips. "Again, we do not know. The only clue we have is one single phrase that comes up time and again: Three Who Are One."

↔

．　．　．

So that was what this was all about. Three Who Are One, a rallying cry I didn't even know existed until Kenji told me about it.

But even I couldn't deny noticing that phrase being thrown around as Others of all types gathered. Still, not all of them were in the let's-get-organized-and-kill-us-some-humans camp. Others like Harry the yeti, who I met at Naha airport, were genuinely on holiday. But this couldn't be a coincidence; whatever drew Harry to Okinawa at this time was the same draw that these homicidal meres were rallying behind.

And all of this somehow connected to where my soul was being held captive, which brought me to another question that had been bothering me from the beginning of all this. When the gods left, my soul was returned to my body the second I became human. But this time around, even though I was only a vampire for a few hours, when I became human once again, my soul never returned. It got stuck somewhere. That didn't make sense … it should have come back like it did the first time, shouldn't it?

"OK," I said thinking of my mystic map. "And you think all this might have something to do with my map."

"We believe that they are looking for the Museum."

"And she believes," Jean said in a way that clearly conveyed the message that he didn't agree, "that your invisible map might lead us to the Museum."

"Bit of a stretch, don't you think? I mean, coincidence much."

"Totally agree," Jean said.

Shouf clicked twice in annoyance. "Coincidence is the weak mind's excuse for not understanding. When you have lived as long as I have, you learn that coincidences are simply connections whose meaning remain hidden."

"And if a tree falls in the forest, and no one is there to hear it, does it make a sound," I said. Shouf, for all her eyelessness, gave me a look that said, 'what the hell are you on about?'

"What?" I said. "You're not the only one who can throw out pointless, unprovable ideas as wisdom."

Jean let out a guffaw that he poorly hid behind the clearing of his throat.

"Besides, you're basing all this on my map," I said holding out my arm that, to them, was as tattooless as a tattooless arm could be. "And for all we know this map is some kind of cosmic joke that's leading me on a wild goose chase."

Jean chuckled again before saying, "Maybe, but whatever is happening is supposed to happen at New Year's. And whatever that event is, the ones in The Three Who Are One camp believe it will lead them to the Museum."

General Shouf nodded in agreement.

"Why? Because they're looking for weapons that can turn the tide of this quiet war," I said, answering my own question.

"Clever girl," Shouf said. I briefly thought about standing up and making good on my earlier threat. But I didn't because the truth was, I did feel clever for figuring it out. "Weapons are only part of it. The appearance of the Kami Subete Hakubutsukan will serve as a rallying cry to other Others to join the fight. But we believe there is more. We believe that within the Kami Subete Hakubutsukan lies a being of power that they believe will lead them to victory," General Shouf's voice shattered.

"The Three Who Are One," Jean said. "In other words, we're in a *Call of Cthulhu* or McGuffin situation."

"You'll have to forgive me, but I don't speak Geek," I said, even though I thought I knew exactly what he was talking about.

"OK," he said, taking his feet off the desk and standing, "*Call of Cthulhu* is the scenario where they're trying to summon a god or powerful Other to lead them. The Three Who Are One. Or maybe they think there's an item inside that place powerful enough to force one or all of the gods back. And if we're in the McGuffin scenario, there's an item in there that represents a god, and whichever Other possesses it will have the street cred to lead the others."

"Either way, it's a unifying front."

"Yep," Jean said. "And El Hefe wants to offer you an indecent proposal."

"Ay, there's the rub," I said.

"More like rug burn," Jean said.

General Shouf clicked twice before saying, "We register you, give you all the resources you need, a very generous salary, equipment, troops, status, power, and you help us find the Kami Subete Hakubut-sukan and stop the impending war or—"

"I'll do it," I said.

"Excuse me?"

"No need for the threats part of your pitch. I'll do it."

"You will?" Jean said, unable to hide the surprise in his voice.

"I will. Now where do I sign?"

15

I REALLY WANTED TO USE THE STICK

"*You're* not even curious about what the threats were?"

Now it was my turn to sigh as if bored. "Let me guess, Jean-*Luc*." The soldier cringed at the second part of his moniker. Man, that guy really hated his name. "You guys are going to hold Egya, Deirdre and Keiko in some kind of Other Guantanamo. If that doesn't get me to comply, then you'll plaster my name all over the place, branding me as a villain, before freezing my assets, getting me kicked out of school and forcing me to move in with my mother."

"Your mother is still alive?"

"Sadly," I said.

"Family, huh? My mother-in-law came back from the dead just to annoy me," he said with a shrug in an I-feel-your-pain kind of way. "But with regard to the threats, you pretty much nailed it. We didn't think of the school part, but the rest is pretty on point. Clever girl." He did a half-decent imitation of General Shouf's voice as he spoke. "Still, as grateful as we are that you so readily want to join our merry band, I'm a little suspicious at how eager you are. So riddle me this: why are you so willing to help us?"

"Who said I'm helping you? There's something there that I want.

Something Eyeballs over there saw—or rather, didn't see—in me. I want my soul back and if you're going to help me get it, then I don't really care about the rest. You can keep whatever else you find in there. Deal?"

Jean looked at General Shouf and I could see the wheels turning. He didn't believe me. Not completely. But in a game of winner takes all, believing me was secondary to getting what they wanted.

General Shouf clicked twice before nodding.

"Great," I said. "Then let's get started. First order of business, free my friends, then let's call up a map or two and try to figure this out."

"Actually," Jean said, standing now, "we have a lead. Got lucky, really. Thanks to you," he added as he pulled out a walkie talkie. "Bring them in."

Then he turned to me. "Seems you're not the only one who knows about the Kami Subete Hakubutsukan." The door into the room opened and in shuffled Kenji and Keiko. "It appears these two also know all about it, too."

↔

The two of them shuffled into the room. Keiko was wearing ankle cuffs that prevented her from taking wide steps and Kenji had a mesh of chains draped over it that slowed down the nurikabe's already awkward gait. They were escorted by two Japanese armed guards that looked like extras in an *Austin Powers* movie—complete with the charcoal-gray caps and uniform. I noted from the way they carried their guns, and how they positioned themselves behind Kenji and Keiko, that these two were clearly well-trained. But despite being professionals, neither looked at Keiko, their attention on the floor behind her.

They were probably thrown off by the disturbing fact that they were guarding a living wall.

Once they were in the center of the room, the guards took three steps back to await further orders.

"Ahh," shattered General Shouf, "our guests have arrived."

"Guests?" Keiko said, giving the aigamuchab a scowl. "Guests do not arrive in chains. HAVE YOU NO DECENCY?"

One of the Japanese guards grimaced as Keiko shouted the words. Apparently he agreed with her that our hosts had no decency.

"Very well," General Shouf said and gestured for the grimacing guard to remove their restraints. The guard did so with unabashed eagerness, first removing Keiko's restraints, then Kenji's.

"Better?" General Shouf shattered.

Keiko knelt and rubbed her ankles. "Marginally," she said with all the defiance of a mountain lion. I saw a lot of Blue's strength in her and feelings of a distant past bubbled to the surface. I knew that I'd protect this girl with the same ferocity I had once protected her grandmother.

"Good," General Shouf said. "Jean, if you will."

"Oh, yeah … OK," Jean said. From the look of him, he had been paying attention to the scene with the detached interest of a man daydreaming about being somewhere else, anywhere else, and General Shouf's undeniable voice brought him back to the present.

He grabbed the remote and showed them the same scene he had shown me: the old news reels, Gabriel's attack, and finally the impending assault on the base.

After that was done, he said, "The fate of the world rests in your hands, yadda, yadda, yadda." When he was done, he tossed the remote down and placed his feet back on the table.

Whoever this guy was, he had a lot of clout for General Shouf to tolerate his insubordination without so much as a word of protest.

And whoever this Jean guy was, his passive-aggressive stance showed me that he clearly did not like what was going on here.

Not that Jean's complete lack of reverence was noted by either Keiko or Kenji. They both stood still, watching the screen, before Keiko said, "Stop the Three Who Are One."

This got Jean's attention. "There it is again. Three Who Are One.

What the hell does it mean and why are Other communities on the island up in arms about it?" Jean narrowed his eyes. "And who are you to know such a word? We've done the tests. You're human. Another ex-vampire?"

Keiko shook her head. "Just one friendly with the Other communities. You should try it sometime—might get what you want without having to wear funny shirts."

"What is it about this shirt? We're on a tropical island, people," Jean said, shrugging off the insult. "OK, so what does it mean?"

"I don't know. But the Others speak of it in hushed tones. From what I know, it refers to something or someone. Either way, whatever it is, most Others are afraid of it."

"And those who aren't afraid?"

"They welcome it," Keiko said.

"Humph. What about you, Mr. Wall?" Jean asked. "Any insights as to what Three Who Are One is?"

Kenji's surface took on a stony exterior.

"Look," Jean said, "we're the good guys. We're the ones trying to stop the big bad from, you know, bad-ing."

"Bad-ing?" I said.

"It's a word. And it means evil spreading, evil maiming, evil killing. Because even though I don't have the slightest clue what Three Who Are One is, I do know that it's not good for anyone. Those meres swimming toward us right now, the mini-army hell-bent on helping their—or his—or her—or its—arrival, they slaughtered a fleet of fishing boats off the Philippine coast a few hours ago. Why? Those boats weren't military and they hadn't spotted them. They couldn't hurt them in any way. But they did it anyway because they got off on it. Given they're the ones that want to meet the Three Who Are One, I'm guessing we're not talking about rainbows and unicorns."

"*Utsuki*," Kenji spat.

"Me, lying?" Jean said, putting a hand on his chest in mock offense. In his hand was the remote, which he clicked. The scene turned to the wreckage of several wooden boats. Even though the cameras were from the ships' bows, we could see several sharks swimming about.

"Nineteen dead. Not a total loss. Two survived by climbing onto some floating debris. They're the ones that told us they were attacked by meres who destroyed their boats and cut them so that their blood would attract the sharks. Evil shit, which makes whatever they're after evil shit, too."

Jean clicked the remote and the screen went blank. "And before you go pointing at us and saying that we're no better, keep in mind that we don't slaughter the innocent."

"Nor do we make any decisions unilaterally," General Shouf said, pointing at the Japanese guards. "As you can see, we are already working with the locals. This is an international effort." She offered an eyeless smile, which came off less friendly and more maniacal monster-ess than anything else. "And all we need is one small thing from you," she said, approaching Kenji. "The location of the Kami Subete Hakubutsukan."

"I don't know what you are talking about," Kenji said.

"Do not lie to me. My soldier said that you showed this girl a location before explaining what the Kami Subete Hakubutsukan was. You know where it is."

"I do not," Kenji said.

General Shouf shrugged, stepping away from the door and grabbing something off the table where Jean's feet so rudely sat. "In all my years wandering the heavens and hells, I have never met a nurikabe before. I have heard of your kind, but to actually stand face-to-face— well, *surface-to-surface*—with you now ... it is an honor. You are truly a rare form of Other. The legendary Obstructer of the Ways and even in this GoneGod World, I see that you live up to your fabled purpose even now."

The aigamuchab stepped closer to the wall, concealing whatever she had picked up. "Japanese myths. What sets them apart from so many other cultures is that they always found magic in the mundane. A demon whose purpose is to wash beans, another whose mischief lies solely in moving one's pillow to cause discomfort, a third who cleans toilets with their tongue and, of course, our dear friend the nurikabe. A living wall." She opened her palm, revealing what was in it.

From where I stood, it looked like Shouf held a key. A simple, plain-looking key and from the way Kenji moved, the wall couldn't have been more afraid. It made sense; Others had weaknesses: silver for weres, crosses for vamps, iron for fae and (apparently) keys for nurikabe.

Kenji shuffled back, and with a nod from General Shouf, the two guards took a step forward, their guns lifted in Kenji's direction.

This got Jean's attention and he stood up, his hand reaching into his back pocket for—what? A gun? A knife? Whatever it was, he kept it there as he readied himself to attack.

"Yamete," Keiko shouted, putting herself between the guards and Kenji.

The guards looked at the young woman, then at General Shouf before lowering their guns.

This sent General Shouf into a rage as she shattered in Japanese, "WHAT ARE YOU DOING? LIFT UP YOUR GUNS."

The aigamuchab spoke the language perfectly, but the guards didn't obey, continuing to keep their rifles at their sides.

Jean didn't hesitate. He pulled out what was in his hand—a pair of cuffs—and in a fluid motion I doubted I would have been capable of as a vampire, let alone a human, struck down the two guards, disarming them before cuffing them. Then he lifted one of their rifles at Keiko. "Whatever mumbo jumbo you used on them won't work on me, missy."

Missy? Did he serious say *missy* in the middle of a fight? Oh, brother.

Time to play diplomat with my fists, I thought as I took a step forward, but before I could get any closer, General Shouf did a round-house kick in my direction. I had expected her to try and knock me down with her heel, and lifted my hands in defense, but at the last second, the aigamuchab took a step forward, the back of her knee connected with my neck, as she twisted, pulling me to the ground.

She was grabbling me with her legs, Scarlett Johansson's Black Widow style. Damn, she was agile. General Shouf (and Scarlett), that is.

On the ground, I cried out, "Hold on, hold on! I'm on your side, remember?" But given the position I was in, the general clearly didn't remember. "I want to find the Kami Subete Hakubutsukan as badly as you. Worse, even," I said.

Neither the general or Jean moved. "Let me talk to Kenji. I'll convince him. And if I can't, then I'll lie down right where you have me now and we can pick up from this spot."

There was a long pause as General Shouf considered this. Then with a click, she let me go. Jean lowered his gun, picked up the other one and pointed for the guards to leave with them.

"You have ten minutes," General Shouf said as she exited the room.

16

WORLD WAR OTHER

"*H*ow could you betray us?" Kenji growled (which, given it was a wall, sounded more like a creak than a roar).

Those words stung me to the core. The last thing I was doing was betraying Kenji. The world was on the brink of war and the only thing standing in the way of that was the morphing map on my arm.

A map that led to an arsenal of magical weapons, which were making the humans very nervous. If the Others got their hands on the place, then the humans would attack without hesitation. But if the humans got there first, then at least they'd be comforted by the knowledge that the Others hadn't gotten their hands on a mythical suitcase nuke.

That might have been enough for the humans to listen to their better angels and not go all out against the Others. And it was the only path I saw to avoiding all-out war.

But I doubted my morphing map would show me the way unless I got closer to the entrance or some event triggered it into a more helpful mode.

I, also, understood where Kenji was coming from. From the nurik-abe's perspective, I was betraying Others. I was choosing a side that wasn't theirs. I was leading the divine into mortal ruin.

And the thought that Kenji could think so little of me really pissed me off, so instead of explaining any of that in a calm, rational way, I spat out, " 'Us?' " I knew exactly what Kenji meant by *us*. "Exactly who do you mean by 'us?' " Angry me and diplomatic me don't speak to each other anymore.

Kenji didn't seem to notice that I was being mordant (or it did and didn't care) because the wall drew a series of thumbnail-sized photos of Others on its surface.

"Oh," I said, "you mean Others. So, what? You think I'm an Other because, once upon a time, I was a vampire? In case you haven't heard, there are no more vampires or werewolves or half-breeds. We're all just human. HUMAN! That's what and who I am now. Human."

The wall went blank in answer, its surface taking on a rock-like texture.

"Oh no, you don't get to stonewall me now. Not with so much at stake. You saw the feeds—you know what's going on. There's a war brewing between Others and humans. A war that neither side can win without major casualties. And if some Other asshole gets access to the museum, said asshole will use whatever is inside to decimate the human race."

"And what do you think humans will do if they get access?" Kenji asked. "Use the items within for benevolent purposes? Turn it into an actual museum? Or will they take every weapon at their disposal and try to kill every Other that stands in their way?"

"At least the humans won't know how to use the items," I said.

"Baka janai?" Kenji spat. "That's your defense? The humans are too stupid to use the items held within Kami Subete Hakubutsukan halls? OK, let us assume that you are correct and that humans are too stupid to figure it out. What about traitors like the aigamuchab? Or is it only stupid Others who betray their own?"

I shook my head. "Kenji, please, they are going to torture you and kill you for the map. Please, tell us what you know, help us find the place. Live. Remember what you told me during the war? You are a survivor. Survive this."

The wall didn't move, its surface becoming more stone-like as if transforming into the outer wall of some medieval castle.

"Kenji, be reasonable. You said it yourself, there are all these foreign Others showing up with seven words on their lips: the Three Who Are One is—are?—coming. You know that's not good. And you know that these Heralds, as you called them, they're looking for the Kami Subete Hakubutsukan as well. Whether the Three Who Are One is a creature or an event, it doesn't matter. The Heralds will use whatever cockamamie scheme they can think of to usher him, her or it in.

"Others and their rituals," I continued. "When did one of those ever happen without a lot of blood being spilled? We could be saving a lot of lives. Other lives. Human lives."

"But the Kami Subete Hakubutsukan will be in human control," Kenji said.

"It will—if we find it. But I have thought this through. Human control is better than Other control because the humans won't know how to use what they find. Think about it: what does a human know about Odin's Eye or how to really use something like that?"

"They will find a way to use such things. They always do."

I shrugged. "Maybe, but the alternative is that it gets into Others' hands ... and those guys *absolutely* know how to use the horrible shit inside for maximum devastation."

Kenji didn't say anything, his surface turing brick red. I tapped Kenji's surface four times like I had done once before when we first met. "Please."

I don't know if it was the familiar way I touched it that brought back memories of when it trusted me, or if it was the comment about survival. Either way, its surface gradually went clear and it revealed the outline of one of the outer islands surrounding Okinawa.

"Here," it said. "This is where legend says the entrance to the Kami Subete Hakubutsukan is located." Kenji's surface showed all of Okinawa and its several outer islands, highlighting an island I'd never seen on any map before. I had a perfect memory and this place was off the charts. Literally.

"Kakusareta Taiyo Shima," it said. "This is the island where Kami

Subete Hakubutsukan is supposed to be, but where on the island, no one knows. But this knowledge will do you no good. This is a sacred island for the noro, a place where no unwelcomed human or Other is permitted. And it is filled with beings and powers who will not take kindly to the human military invading their home. Go. Go and die."

Maybe, I thought, *but no one else has a mystic, invisible map tattooed to their arm.*

Then again, if he was right about the Others on the island, then map or no, there wasn't much hope.

"No," Keiko said, "she will not die. She will have me."

↔

"Keiko," the wall said, "please stay out of this. There is no need for you to place yourself in danger. Think of your grandmother. Think of—"

"It is precisely because of grandmother that I offer this service," she said. "I will be your guide and protect you as you search for Kami Subete Hakubutsukan."

I looked at the five-foot-nothing, wafer-thin girl. "I appreciate the offer," I said, "and your driving skills aside, how exactly will you protect me?" I knew I was being a hypocrite given I, too, was five-foot-nothing.

Keiko bowed and said with reverence, "My grandmother grew up in this world and in Yomi. Those doorways were opened to us because of Kenji-sama. My grandmother spent a lifetime sharing our culture with them and they, in turn, shared theirs with us." Keiko pulled what looked like a handkerchief from her pocket and placed it around her forehead.

I didn't need her to tell me what the cloth represented or who she was. I had seen that white cloth worn in exactly the same manner before, at the end of the war.

Keiko was a noro.

. . .

↔

Keiko was a noro, which made perfect sense. It was why the Okinawan guards had refused to point their guns at her. It was also why she was immediately notified when we entered Kenji's izakaya.

She was an Okinawan priestess for a religion that had been struggling to maintain its traditions since World War II, when mainland Japanese soldiers outlawed their language and religious practices, doing their damndest to erase that part of the island's culture.

Noro priestesses carried immense respect, officiating all aspects of life from blessing births to performing final rites at death. But it was more than that: they also stood between the mystical and human worlds. When a yokai terrorized the mortal realm, noro were called to help. And when a human somehow offended the divine ... well, noro were there to defend the hapless mortal.

Their religion was never about worshipping gods, per se. It had more to do with respecting the unseen world of the yokai; they saw these Others as part of the natural order of things that existed in parallel with the human world.

And they were female, which was refreshing given that ninety-nine percent of world religions were dominated by men.

Now that the gods were gone, it made perfect sense that the priestesses' role would be more pronounced. After all, the line between Others and humans was blurring, and that fuzziness was only getting more and more confusing as Others tried to figure out how to be mortal.

Given that they had always served as mediators between the divine and mortal worlds, not much had changed for them. Except now the yokai were a physical presence who needed help with more mundane matters, like getting a lease or figuring out how to operate their oven. The noro had international respect amongst Other communities, species and sects, and what had once been a dying religion was reinvigorated with renewed interest and deference.

Now it was my turn to bow to Keiko. "I had no idea."

"My family has had so many blessings because of what you did for us. It will be my honor to aid you."

"Keiko," Kenji said, "the humans cannot get their hands on what the Kami Subete Hakubutsukan holds."

"I do not know if I agree with you, my old friend. There is wisdom in what Kattorina-sama says. Both sides will use the Kami Subete Hakubutsukan for evil, and it is only a matter of time until the halls are found by one group or the other. The humans will not know how to use what is inside, and control of the place may very well be what the world needs to forge peace."

"I do not agree," Kenji said. "I believe that—"

An explosion shook the room we were standing with such force that both Keiko and I both fell over.

Kenji nearly fell on Keiko, but I managed to get my footing in time to dash to her side and prop the nurikabe up. He was surprisingly light for a wall.

"Seems the time for discussion is over," a voice shattered as General Shouf entered the room. "Now is the time to act."

End of Part 2

PART III
INTERMISSION

17

OKINAWA - WORLD WAR II

ecades ago—

Just what I need, I thought, *a little human brat who's too cute to eat.*

"Eat-to?" the little girl said.

"Eat-to?" I repeated, immediately regretting that I had thought that out loud. Thankfully the little human couldn't speak English and I had only thought out loud in English … I think.

"Eat-to," she repeated and raised a cupped hand to her mouth like she was scooping water from a river. Then she touched her belly and gave me a groan that clearly said, *"If you're here to take care of me, then take care of me. And FYI, I could eat."*

The little brat was hungry. Hell, I was hungry. And given that she was my food, I could kill two birds with one pair of fangs. Me—no longer hungry. Little girl—no longer anything.

As I looked down at those big brown eyes, considering how good she'd taste, I shook my head. She wasn't food. I had decided that when I saved her from a quick death by a bullet. To kill her now would be cruel, and although I was an evil, human-eating vampire, I wasn't cruel.

Never cruel.

I lifted a *one minute, please* finger. *"Chotomatte kudasai,"* I said, and left the cave looking for food for me and the little brat.

↔

I returned an hour or so later with rations I had taken from a Japanese soldier who was foolish enough to think he could eat in peace in the Okinawan brush. Poor guy. Then again, I'd seen that his bento box— definitely not army issue—had goya inside, and I put two and two together.

He'd stolen it from a farmer. Probably killed the poor guy for his lunch.

So I stole it back and had a little nibble of my own.

The little girl scooped the lunch box out of my hand and ate its contents with such fervor that I began to wonder if she didn't plan to stop with the goya and might eat the woven bamboo of the box itself.

When she was done, she looked at me, her hunger subsided enough for her to notice that my little food hunt had gotten me shot. A bullet hole had ripped the gingham dress I'd gotten from Harrods a few years back. I lamented the damaged dress because, given how much bombing the Germans were doing, Harrods—let alone London —probably wasn't even standing anymore.

She poked a finger through the hole, feeling the still wet blood on my shirt. She moved her finger around the hole, looking for my wound and when she didn't see any, she lowered her hand. This wasn't the first time she'd seen me wounded. Hell, she'd practically watched as I burst into flames from exposure to sunlight.

But that had been just after watching her parents die. Now was different. Now she had some distance. Some clarity. And that clarity caused her eyes to widen as she looked at me with abject horror. *"Yokai,"* she said.

↔

Yokai, the Japanese word for demon. Boy, it didn't take her long to peg me for exactly what I was.

I had expected her to run or cry or fall to her knees and beg in a fury of multisyllabic words, but she didn't do any of that. Instead, she stood before me and bowed deeply, a sign of extreme respect. I didn't know it at the time, but the Okinawans' approach to demons was one of fear that was tempered by respect, accepting them as part of the natural order of things.

Westerners tended to just go for the fear. And as for acceptance, well, the Bible is filled with examples of prophets and heroes chasing demons away from the mortal plane.

As a vampire, I much preferred the Japanese way of doing things.

The little brat was still bowing and I put a gentle hand on her chin, lifting her face until our eyes met. *"Yokai,"* I confirmed, putting a hand on my chest. *"Watashi no namae wa* Katrina Darling."

"Kattorina Daruringu," she said, somewhat butchering my name with the Japanese absolute obsession with adding syllables to everything. She bowed again, this time pointing at herself. "Aoi Uehara."

Humph, her name translated to Blue High-field. Hell of a name.

Then again, mine was Cat Loved One (well, sort of), so I guess it made sense we got along.

I bowed to the child, calling her Aoi-chan—*chan* being the common moniker for the young—before pointing at the sky. "You know, Aoi means blue in English." The child tilted her head as she tried to comprehend a language that she'd probably never heard spoken before. So I said it in Japanese. *"Aoi wa eggo ni wa 'blue' desu."*

"Buru?"

"Close enough," I said before poking her nose. "From now on I'm going to call you Blue Sky. No, that's not right—how about just Blue?"

"Buru," she said, a little more smoothly now. As it dawned on her that I'd just given her a new nickname, her face beamed as she giggled.

I swear to everything we vampires hold holy that I felt my dead heart beat within my chest when I saw that beautiful child's grin.

↔

Over the next few weeks, Blue and I found a rhythm. I ate naughty soldiers (she never let me eat the good ones) and stole their food for her.

It was June 1945. I didn't need to see the news to know that the war was wrapping up.

During the last days of the war, the U.S. Army was sweeping through Okinawa, fighting the remaining soldiers who couldn't accept they had lost. But for the most part, there was very little fighting, with most choosing to surrender to the inevitable.

Unfortunately, surrender didn't always mean a white flag and your hands up in the air. Often, surrender meant death.

And that's exactly what happened. Soldiers and civilians alike committed suicide. Soldiers did so by fighting a battle that could only end one way. Civilians did so by taking their own lives rather than being captured by the *gaijin* barbarian hordes.

Of course, it didn't help that soldiers (falsely) spread rumors that the American soldiers would torture and rape you, subject you to worse kinds of humiliation. That being taken in by these monsters was not only a fate worse than death, it was also a betrayal of everything you once stood for.

I'm not here to paint a pretty picture of the invading American army. They did horrible, unforgivable acts during that war. But they weren't the monsters the rumors made them out to be. If anything, they were trying to stabilize things by setting up internment camps that offered food and shelter to anyone who would take it.

But when it's been drilled into your head that evil is coming and you've been told that nothing will save you from the horrors that evil has in store for you, and when those messages come on the heels of defeat after years of war ... well, the end doesn't sound all that bad.

It sounds peaceful, even.

Of course, Blue and I didn't know any of that while wandering the tropical forests of Okinawa. All we knew was that American boots on the ground meant the war was ending, and that end meant that Blue needed a home.

A home I stupidly thought I'd found one evening near an abandoned goya field a few miles outside of Naha.

18

BOOM, BOOM, SHAKE, SHAKE
THE ROOM

resent Day—

Leaving Kenji behind, Jean led us through the base, rushing toward the corridors of the bunker. "What's going on?" I said.

Jean led us down an underground passageway that connected bunkers and buildings on the base. Below was a maze of gray-painted walls and acronyms I didn't understand. We ran until we hit a junction that led up a stairwell labeled *A.O.A.*

"A.O.A.?" I asked.

"Anti-Other Armory," he said, opening a door with a passkey and leading us into a warehouse with row after row of shelves filled with stuff that hurt, incapacitated or outright killed Others.

Jean put a backpack on a metal table and started filling it. "Seems the eggheads didn't calculate currents or burning time when estimating the meres' arrival." Jean stuffed the backpack to the brim before slinging it over his shoulders. "Supplies and gizmos," he offered by way of explanation.

Then he pulled out two pistols, another shotgun and a duffel bag of ammo. He didn't give any of that stuff to us. He did, however, toss us telescopic steel batons. *I guess beggars can't be choosers,* I thought.

"I guess this means we're—how do you boys put it?—shipping out."

Jean nodded. "Yep, but shipping out is navy. I'm not navy."

"That's right, you're not navy. You're also not army. So what are you, exactly?"

"I'm part of the Kickass Armed Forces, First Division," he said with a grin, gesturing for us to keep moving.

"How quaint," I said. "But I'm not taking another step until you answer a few questions."

Jean sighed. "Fine. Shoot."

"Interesting choice of words," I said. "First, where's Kenji and what's going to happen to it?"

"The wall's safe."

"Kuso," Keiko spat.

"No shit, Little Miss Noro. I know all about your kind and the last thing I'd want to offend is one of the last bastions of the divine on Earth."

Keiko just scowled as she searched his words for a lie. Evidently she didn't find one, because she eventually nodded.

That was enough for me. "Good," I said. "And my friends?"

"Safe. They're being transported off base to a safe house as we speak."

I stomped my foot in a very literal 'digging in of heels' way. "No siree Bob. They're coming with us."

"Nope," Jean said. "I'm afraid that their release is conditional on you keeping your end of the bargain."

"You don't understand what an asset they'll be on the battlefield. Egya is an expert hunter and Deirdre is a changeling—as in, a badass warrior fae changeling. We'll need them should things get hairy."

"I'm all the assets you'll need," Jean said, and I saw that he wasn't being arrogant; he was simply stating a fact. "Your friends are safe and getting first-class treatment. Scout's honor." he lifted three fingers in a Scout's salute. I had no doubt this guy was an Eagle Scout all the way.

"And ma'am," he continued, "I cannot emphasize this enough: we've got to get going."

"Look, stop calling me ma'am. I'm too young to be a ma'am."

"You're over three hundred years old," he said.

"I'm still not a ma'am." Another explosion sounded above us. "So, you said something about shipping out?"

↔

Jean led us outside, where the fighting was in full force. For a base preparing for an onslaught of mermaids and mermen, they certainly weren't prepared for fliers.

Dragons loomed over the base, diving down and using their breath weapons. I watched as a red dragon released fire along the landing strip, enveloping several fighter planes and the pilots who were trying to get the metal birds off the ground.

A blue dragon sent a bolt of electricity at the control tower and I watched with horror as the lights went out and the structure buckled under the heat of the lightning.

And it wasn't just dragons. At the far end of the field where the supply ships had been, a legion of valkyrie were engaging soldiers in hand-to-hand combat. That is, if you could call what was happening "hand to hand." The valkyrie all wielded swords and were slicing through soldiers like they were playing a game of *Fruit Ninja*.

"This way," screamed Jean, pausing as a yellow dragon flew overhead.

I had just enough time to wonder what yellow dragons breathed before it opened its mouth and vomited lava over several parked Humvees. *Seriously*, I thought, *lava?* No wonder the humans were scared.

"So," I said to Jean as he opened the door to one of the Humvees that hadn't just been puked on by a volcano, "I'm guessing the attack on the fleet was a diversion." Then turning to Keiko, asked, "I don't suppose your noro clout will be of use here?"

She shook her head and said, *"Gaijin."*

Foreigners.

Yep, that about summed it up. These Others weren't of the Japanese variety and would respect an order from a noro priestess just about as much as they would an order from Captain Crunch.

With a sigh, we jumped into the Humvee and sped off.

↔

Jean drove like a bat out of hell, dodging breath weapons and hurled swords as he made his way through the base's open area.

"Where are we going?" I asked.

"To the ship," he said. "But first I'm going to slay me a dragon."

"Really?" I said, skeptical as I watched the red, yellow and blue dragons circle as they coordinated their next attack.

Jean sped the car away from the base and toward the shipyard on the other side of the base, well away from the action. It seemed like an old repair yard and from the looks of it, hadn't been active for decades.

From the sight of all the Kanji, I gathered that this was actually a Japanese repair yard they'd probably used during the war and, because it had been one of their bases, the Americans had taken it over afterward.

Because we were away from the action, the dragons and valkyrie left us alone, figuring we were running away. Hell, I figured we were running away until Jean slammed on the brakes and jumped out of the car.

We followed as he climbed up the ladder of a wooden ship. "You know that the Japanese are some of the fiercest whale hunters on the planet?" he said, pulling at a tarp to reveal a harpoon big enough to impale a bus. "This puppy is probably a hundred years old. I've been fixing it up," he said, rubbing his hands along its exterior and patting it like a treasured pet. "Oiling it, replacing parts. Totally on my own time and dime. You see, I have a thing for old toys."

He pulled at the gears, putting in a harpoon-cannon he'd pulled from a nearby crate. The harpoon, unlike its cannon, didn't look to be old at all. For one thing, it was shiny and well-polished. For another, its tip beeped.

Jean pointed it at the yellow dragon, looked at his watch (which I noted was one of those old Mickey Mouse watches from back in the day) and muttered, "No magic," before releasing the harpoon. The missile flew true, and it stuck the yellow dragon in the soft part where its wing met its body.

The yellow dragon grimaced in pain, but it didn't go down, reacting more like one would when stung by a bee than impaled by a needle with a three-inch-wide tip. The dragon looked in our direction, flapping its wings as it flew toward us.

"Shit," I yelled. "We've got to run."

Jean shook his head. "Nah. You see, I also have a thing for things that go boom." And as if it had heard him, the harpoon exploded and the dragon went down like a pheasant in a shoot.

It didn't matter that I'd just watched that dragon spew lava; it hurt to watch a creature like that drop so ingloriously. It hit the ground with a thud so massive the ship beneath us shook.

"One down, two to go," Jean said, putting in another harpoon and aiming at the red dragon. But dragons aren't dumb; this one had seen Yellow go down and was ready. It dodged the harpoon, swooping to the left at the last second.

And I secretly hoped Red would make it, even if that meant it would come after us.

But the dragon's evasive maneuvers didn't do any good. The harpoon exploded as soon as it was next to Red and the blast was strong enough to send that dragon to the ground, too.

Jean shook his head. "They just caught us off guard, that's all," he said, more to himself than us. I thought he'd load a third harpoon, but he didn't, just staring ahead.

Turning, I watched as several soldiers ran out of the bunker with shoulder RPGs and sent a barrage of missiles at the blue dragon. Their aim wasn't as good as Jean's and the explosive power wasn't quite the same grade as his harpoons, but the sheer volume of the attack was enough to take the last dragon down.

In the distance, the last of the valkyrie was being taken down by machine gun fire as several of her compatriots took to the sky to escape. But they were also being picked off one by one by surface-to-air missiles from several tanks rolling onto the field.

I looked over at Keiko, who watched in horror as the whole scene unfolded. Her eyes were wide open as she took in everything. She spoke to herself as she watched the human soldiers manage to get themselves together and repel the attacks.

I didn't need to lean in close to hear what she was saying. Her misting eyes told me exactly what she murmured: a prayer for the dead and dying.

↔

We got into the Humvee and made our way back to where the fighting had been heaviest. As we got closer, I saw that the red dragon was still alive, its body badly mangled by the harpoon blast and fall, but also by several soldiers who were taunting it, taking turns stabbing it with Ka-Bars and bayonets. I'd seen this behavior before. In the fog of war, torturing your enemy became somehow acceptable because—well, who was going to stop you? There was a justification to punishing your enemy, an evil catharsis in making sure their last moments were spent in pain.

Besides, it was a dragon. To them that meant a beast—a non-thinking, non-feeling animal. But dragons were some of the smartest creatures on the planet, not that I could convince any one of these soldiers of that.

Jean sped up to the horrific scene. "Seriously," I said, "it's not enough that you destroyed that creature. Now you want to take part in the after-party, too?"

"You think you know me," he said as he slammed the brakes, "but you don't know shit."

He got out of the truck and walked over to a soldier that was approaching the beast, a maniacal grin on his face. Without hesitation, I heard Jean say, "You think this is fun?" before punching the soldier square in the nose. Two other soldiers jumped Jean and I got out, kicking one of them in the chin before giving the other guy a well-placed punch in the center of his back.

Both of them went down, but then five more jumped in. Now it was Keiko who showed up, kicking one of them in the nose before doing some serious Krav Maga grappling with another. The two went down with a crunch.

This might have digressed into a full-on bar fight had it not been for an immaculately dressed older man who came onto the scene screaming with an obviously well-practiced battlefield voice. "Enough!"

We all stopped fighting.

"Don't you all have somewhere to be? Clean up time, boys," he yelled, sending everyone running.

Everyone but Jean, Keiko and me.

"And as for you," the commander said, looking at Jean, "why is it that every time there's a fight, it usually involves you defending one of these—these demons?"

Jean didn't say anything, walking right up to the commander until their faces were an inch apart. Even though the commander didn't back off, his expression unchanged, I could smell the fear on him (an ex-vampire thing; I can tell a lot about people from the way they smell). This guy was afraid of Jean, and after seeing how he'd taken down two dragons, I got it. I was starting to fear this Jean-Luc Matthias, too.

"I don't know, Captain Donnelly," Jean said, "maybe because they're not demons, and I still have my soul?"

Jean moved forward, which caused the commander to flinch, and in that distracted second, Jean took the commander's pistol from its holster. Showing the man his own gun, Jean said, "If you don't mind."

He stepped over to the dragon who was clearly in pain. The dragon reared its head, trying to get away from Jean, and that's when the human did the last thing I expected him to do.

He started to sing.

I recognized the song; it was an ancient Celtic song about the fall of night. I'd heard Deirdre sing it before at a funeral. The dragon stopped trying to crawl away and turned its head to face Jean. There, I saw acceptance as the human soldier stood close enough to the dragon's jaws that it could have easily killed him, wounded or not.

But it didn't. Instead it remained there as Jean continued the song. And when he was done, the dragon closed his eyes as Jean put the pistol against the soft part of its neck, where the spine met the back of its brain stem, and pulled the trigger.

The dragon died in an instant, its death painless and quick. Jean patted the dragon's lifeless head. "Sorry it had to be this way."

Damn, vicious and compassionate, I thought. In another life he would have been my kind of guy.

Not now. Now I tended to go just for compassionate.

Jean tossed Captain Donnelly his pistol. "Ship ready?"

The captain holstered his gun and pointed at a twelve-foot speed boat with three sailors on it. "It survived the attack."

"Good." Jean gestured for us to get on the boat.

The commander gave Jean a salute. "Godspeed."

Jean gave a halfhearted salute back, not even looking at the man. "Yeah, yeah," Jean said. "Speed of god and all that."

And with that, we boarded the ship and sped off into the darkness of the sea.

19

BLACK HOLE SEA, WON'T YOU COME AND DROWN AWAY THE PAIN?

*A*s soon as the ship left the war-torn base, Keiko went below deck to meditate, leaving Jean and me to stand at the front of the ship, not talking, just watching the darkness approach but never get closer. It just kept going, and I wondered if this was an omen for what was to come.

Then again, it could just be because it's night, I thought.

"Excuse me?" Jean said.

"Private thoughts. It's a quirk of mine … I think out loud. A lot."

Jean gave me a knowing look. "So it mentions in your file. Not that I'm surprised. A lot of vamps—well, *ex*-vamps—do. I guess it comes from spending centuries wandering this world alone."

He spoke as if he knew me, and not just from a file, but really knew me. I don't know if it was the tone, or everything that had just happened, but his familiarity annoyed me. And rather than taking the high road, I growled in just about the most childish tone I could muster, "You don't know me." Impulse control much, Kat?

"You're right—I don't. But I'm starting to, and I like what I see." He lifted his hand before I could say anything. "And I don't mean in a 'what's your sign, come here often?' kind of way. You care, Kat. And you do something about it. Too many care but do nothing. And way, way, way too many simply don't care."

"Sounds like you figured me out," I said in a sarcastic tone, and because I spent so much time with Deirdre and other Others, I figured it would go over his head like it did them. But Jean was human.

Humans get sarcasm.

"You're right," he said, "it is presumptuous of me to think I know you. I'm sorry."

I felt bad. Here he was trying to reach out and I'd shot him down. So, turning around and finding the exit for the high road, I softened my voice. "I'm not the only one who cares."

"Oh yeah, and what evidence do you have of that? Was it the two dragons I killed today that tipped you off?" He turned to look out at the sea again, as if the ever-approaching darkness would hide his shame.

"You're a soldier defending your base. The way I see it, you had no choice."

Jean shook his head and shrugged. "I don't know. Bella would say there is always a choice," he said, his voice trailing off.

Who's Bella? I wondered, but instead of saying anything else, he just kept looking out over the sea.

I thought the conversation was over, but he broke the silence with a heavy sigh. "I'm probably going to regret this, but since we're two individuals with questionable people skills, I have a proposal. We each get to ask the other a question, and we both have to promise to answer the question honestly."

"A question for a question?"

"With an honest answer for an honest answer," he emphasized.

I nodded and stuck out my hand. He didn't take it, instead saying, "Back in the interrogation room you said that you didn't want our forgiveness because you'll never forgive yourself. What did you mean exactly?"

"Isn't it obvious?"

"I had assumed that you mean forgiving yourself for killing as a vampire, but I've met a lot of your kind. Hell, half of the special forces are ex-vamps. Those guys don't seem to be bothered by killing. And not one of them ever expressed regret. So …" he let the last word linger.

"I hate myself for all the lives I took—"

He lifted a scolding finger. "Honest answer, remember?"

"You're worse than Mergen. The truth … fine. Here it is: as a vampire I must have killed dozens of humans, and almost every single one of them I hunted down in some perverted cat-and-mouse game. I was the damsel in distress. 'Oh mister, I must get home but the way there is so dark. I'm afraid. You're big and strong. Will you be a gentleman and escort me?' " I mimicked a dainty girl calling for help. "I also played the huntress, giving my prey a full minute's head start. And then there was the temptress. My favorite, because back then I was a fifteen-year-old girl and the way I figured it, any guy willing to take me to bed deserved to die."

Jean gave me a questioning look.

"And yes, before you ask, the gentlemen who turned me down did get to live. Most of them, anyway. But that's not my point. My point is I enjoyed killing and now that I'm human again, I hate it. I hate that part of me.

"Not the killing, mind you. That bothers me, but I can accept that it was kill or die. That part of being a vampire was somehow justifiable. It was the part of me that *enjoyed* the killing. That's the part I'll never forgive because, even though I'm human again, I still love the hunt." I looked up at Jean. "Was that truth enough for you?"

"Yeah."

"Your turn."

"You know, I'm more of a dare guy."

"Ah, ah, ah." I waggled a finger. "We had a deal."

He groaned. "Fine. What's your question?"

"Who are you?"

"Humph." He smiled. "That's easy. I'm Jean."

My face went stoic as I waited patiently for the answer.

"Jean-Luc Matthias. And before you make the joke—yes, I am only missing the Mark. Ha-ha."

I made it painfully obvious that I didn't get the joke—if there was one in there to begin with.

"You know," he explained, "Jean-Luc Matthias. John, Luke and Matthew. From the gospels, but I'm missing the Mark. Again, ha-ha."

"You know, you're not very funny."

"I am in Paradise Lot," he muttered.

"And you're not keeping your end of the bargain. Who are you?"

"I don't know what you mean."

"Yes you do," I said. "You've spent enough time with Others to know exactly what I mean. And as a former Other, I mean it in *that* way. Who are you?"

I was certain he knew what I was doing. When an Other asked you who you were, they weren't searching for a name or race, creed or species. They were asking you to unveil every aspect of who you were. They were asking to know you like you knew yourself.

Sure, you might not know who you are. Not fully. But if you were to answer the question honestly, you were on the hook to voice every conclusion you'd ever come to when reflecting on who you were.

He paused, understanding and regret painting his face. "Clever girl," he said, "packing so much into one question like that."

Oh boy, back to the "clever girl" stuff.

"So?" Now it was my turn to let the word linger.

"Very well. I'm human. Not a drop of anything else in me. When the gods left, they killed my grandfather. Sure, it was an accident caused by the confusion of the gods' departure, but it doesn't change the fact that he's dead because of them.

"So I picked up a weapon and joined the fight, and discovered that I'm damn good at it. I don't get scared. I don't clam up. I just do whatever it takes to bring my targets down. It was like these hands were meant for killing. So who am I? I am anger. I am vengeance. And I'm amazing at it."

He stopped talking and I thought that might have been everything. That this man's entire self-reflection boiled down to one thing: hate.

But then he sighed, touching his wedding ring. "But the best part of me isn't what I think of myself. It's what she thinks of me. She keeps saying that I am love and compassion, and she's said it enough times that I'm starting to believe her. So because of her, I am vengeance and compassion. I am anger and forgiveness. In other words, I'm fucked up."

"Aren't we all?" I said. "I think that's what it means to be human."

We stood together for a long moment, staring into the darkness of the sea. Two fucked up humans trying to find our way. We might not have been friends, but we shared the unbreakable bond of trying to be something we weren't.

"So, Bella. She's who you were referring to?"

He nodded. "And who's Mergen? Boyfriend?"

"Nope. He's my friend, the Avatar of Truth and a pain in the ass."

"I get that," Jean said.

"So," I said, "now that we've bared our souls to each other, what happens next?"

"Now we get to the island, find the museum before Three Who Are One arrive—whatever or whoever they are—and cross our fingers that the skirmishes stop."

"Sounds like a pl—" I started, when the ship rocked.

Not rocked—stopped. The abrupt halt sent us both tumbling toward the front of the ship with such force that I fell off. I now know why the expression "man (or in this case, woman) overboard" is a thing.

As I hurtled toward the black sea, I felt a hand grab me. Jean. As he hoisted me back onto the boat, I looked down to see several eyes staring back at me.

And not just any eyes. These were ones with catlike vertical slits.

Meres. Yay!

20

MERES AND AN UNDERWATER GRIFFIN

*M*ost people think of mermaids and mermen as these half-human, half-fish creatures, their human halves being especially beautiful and, more often than not, naked. It's also commonly believed that meres are these benevolent, playful creatures who save fishermen from drowning and help lost ships find their way home. You know, like dolphins with six packs and boobs. I blame movies like *Splash* and *The Little Mermaid* for these misconceptions.

For one thing, meres' upper torsos don't look at all human, with greenish-blue fish scales covering their (admittedly) naked chests. Their eyes are catlike in nature, with long vertical slits designed to see in near total darkness. Their ears look like lionfish fins or paper fans, where the flaps of skin not only help them hear underwater, but also detect vibrations in what is otherwise the silent deep. They have a series of vertical slits where their noses should be that are more gills than nostrils, and their mouths … well, the phrase, "What big teeth you have, Grandmother" comes to mind.

The last thing about them is that they're never alone, choosing to travel in—what do you call a group of meres? A school, like fish? Given their size and humanoid nature, I'm going to go for a *school bus* of meres. (Here's to coining the phrase.)

Regardless of the correct terminology, meres travel in packs. And they hunt in packs. There's a reason why those familiar with meres call them the wolves of the sea.

Jean yelled at the driver to start up again and the engines roared to life. Not that it mattered. The meres just swam along with us, easily circling the speed boat despite us going at top speed. So I guess I needed to add "incredibly fast" to their list of abilities.

"Shit," I said as Jean pulled me up onto the boat's deck. "They're everywhere."

Jean looked over the edge and shrugged. "At least they're not a school of myarids," he said, taking this latest development in stride. "Those guys are truly vicious."

"Good. I'm glad you're able to see the bright side of things, but myarids or meres—either way, they're going to try to drown us." As if agreeing with me, the boat rocked as several meres rammed into its side.

Keiko came out of the cabin. She held two telescopic batons and tossed me one. *"Nani da?"*

"Meres," I said, looking over the edge, careful not to expose too much of myself. I had no idea how high they could jump out of the water and I had an image of myself being dragged under by a particularly spry one.

There was another bang and the boat swayed back and forth as it sped forward. The tilting was strong enough that the boat was taking on quite a bit of water.

Two of the sailors came out, their faces washed with fear. They each held a shotgun and they immediately started shooting over the edge. They didn't even bother aiming; they just blasted into the darkness of the sea.

Jean, on the other hand, went below deck to ... who knows? He was taking the whole scene so casually that part of me wondered if he'd gone below for a nap.

Without a shotgun, I was of little use standing where I was. Keiko must have gotten the same idea because she pocketed her baton and went to the front of the boat to ... sing. As in, literally singing. As in

I'm-auditioning-for-*American-Idol* singing. She sang some strange song at the top of her lungs, something in the local Okinawan dialect, ancient and melodic. Beautiful really, and I might have put down a picnic blanket to listen if we weren't under attack.

Looking at the singing noro, I figured that either the fear of drowning had caused her to go nuts or she had the most awkward nervous tic ever.

Seeing she was of no use, I decided to stop standing around twiddling my thumbs and join the driver on the bridge of the boat. I turned the two searchlights on, giving the soldiers some light to help with the shooting.

Not that they needed it. There were so many meres that every shot was bound to hit something.

But the light did illuminate another problem. Even though every spray of bullets struck the meres, they did little damage. There was no blood in the water and the meres showed no signs of trying to avoid the shots.

Fan-friggin-tastic, I thought. This was useless. I looked around the deck for something, anything to help repel the attack. Then an idea inspired by the spotlights hit me: what do meres hate more than terrible movies that don't represent them at all?

Fire. At least, I suspected as much. I mean, they spent their lives in cool water, so heat must have bothered them.

I ran down into the cabin, digging through its bowels until I found what I was looking for. What I didn't find was a Jean. His backpack was lying around, but after rummaging through it, I found little of use for a battle with meres. Other fun stuff, sure, but a school bus of meres required something a little bit more "ouchy."

Scanning the deck below, I finally found what I was looking for: a canister of gasoline and a flare gun.

Things were starting to look up.

↔

. . .

The boat rocked again and from the tilt, I figured that the meres were slamming into us from the right side. Another boom and this time the boat tilted so violently that one of the soldiers went over with a scream that abruptly ended as the meres pulled him under. Poor kid.

Not that I had time to think about that now. Running over to the right side, I looked over the edge and poured the gasoline so that it cascaded down the boat's metal side and into the water. I waited for the ramming meres to return and as soon as they were close, I let loose the flare gun.

The side went up in flames as the meres leapt out of the water to ram us again. But instead of hitting slick, cool metal, they were greeted by a wall of fire that sent them back to the water with a yelp.

The side of the boat was on fire, offering us a "mere shield" of sorts for all of three seconds before the meres splashed the sides, dousing the flames.

I shook the canister. There was enough fuel to repeat my trick once more, possibly twice before they would be back to the old tactic of boat-tipping.

Looking around for something, anything to better our chances, I saw that Keiko still stood at the front of the boat, continuing her strange song. Her singing was barely audible above the roar of the engine and the rush of the wind.

Still, though, I could hear the words clearly (not that I understood them), recognizing them as Hoogan, the local Okinawan language that was slowly dying as the older generation passed into the good night.

"Damn it," I screamed over the roar of engines and wind as I did my fire trick one last time. "Damn it, damn it, damn it!" My last cry was deafening to my own ears because as I yelled out, the engines suddenly went silent and the boat came to an abrupt halt.

And here was me thinking that things couldn't get worse.

↔

. . .

"Sorry about that," Jean said, coming out from the bow dragging two wires behind him. One of the wires was in his hand while the other one seemed to be attached to his back pocket.

"Sorry about what?" I said.

Jean looked behind him at Keiko. "What's she doing?"

"Singing," I said. "And don't deflect. What are you sorry about?"

"Stopping the boat. But I was getting sea sick and—"

"You stopped the boat?" I screamed. "Are you insane? Or suicidal?"

"Miral said I'm both, that I suffer from something called Moral Madness. Personally, I think it's a made-up condition—"

The meres banged into our side, but because the boat was no longer moving, it had settled into the water and the tilt was far less than it had been before.

"Then again, if I was insane," Jean continued, not missing a beat, "I probably wouldn't know it." He dragged the wires to the boat's edge and looked at my shoes. "Good, you're wearing sneakers."

"They're not sneakers," I said. "They're Balenciaga Race Runners." I could hear the meres gathering in close and a light clanging coming from the boat's exterior. From the systematic chimes they were making, I gathered they weren't going to ram us again. Instead, they were looking for the weakest point to dig a big hole into. They were trying to sink us.

"They're sneakers," Jean said. He pointed behind him toward the driver and remaining soldier. "They're in army-issue boots and Little Miss Sunshine over there is in tennis shoes." He draped the wire over the edge and called out, "Keep your hands to yourself. No touching railings, please."

"Why? What are you doing—?"

But before I could finish, he pulled out the second wire from his back pocket. It had a clamp at the end like one of those car battery jacks. Then I took a closer look and saw that that was exactly what it was: a jack.

He attached the metal crocodile teeth onto the railing as sparks electrified the edge. "These aren't your typical boat batteries. They're souped-up, army-issue developed by Memnock Securities for exactly this kind of scenario." His face was lit up by the sparks. "In other words, they're bad ass."

I looked over the edge, where electricity crackled through the water as blue waves of hot lightning. The meres who were closest to the boat were burned, their skin melting underwater. They were the first to dart away in pain.

The other meres who were lucky enough to be far enough away circled the blue flames from a safe distance.

Jean released the jack and the illuminated water went black again. "There's plenty more of that," he yelled over the edge. "Don't believe me? Come in close and see." He sat down with his back to the edge of the railing.

"Pretty cool," I said. "What's the plan now?"

Jean shook his head. "Not sure. That was all the juice we had and it will only be a matter of time until they decide to try again. We could call for help, but they're hours away. We might get lucky that the electrical burns were severe enough to keep them at bay until help comes."

He looked over at Keiko, who continued singing. She had a pleasant enough voice given that she was screaming the song at the top of her lungs.

"Who knows?" Jean said. "Maybe her singing will drive them away."

↔

Jean wasn't wrong. Keiko's singing did drive the meres away, but not because they didn't like her song. They didn't like what her song summoned.

About twenty minutes after we stopped, there was a loud rustling as the water's surface became disturbed. We heard screaming in the mere language and, looking over the side, I watched as several meres were knocked out of the water like killer whales did to seals they were tormenting.

Keiko came over, watching the scene with a pleased smile on her face. "Makara," she said.

Jean nodded, "You can call one?" Then answering his own question, said, "Of course you can. The Hindu mythological creatures still believe in the divine, don't they? I mean, after centuries of worshipping dozens of gods, what's one more to them? And given you guys are one of the few remaining functioning religions ... Say, you don't want a job, do you?"

In answer, Keiko looked at the soldier with disdain.

"I figured," he said, "but it never hurts to ask."

The scene continued unfolding for another few minutes, but eventually the splashing and screaming subsided as the makara drove away the school bus (see, it's catching!) of meres.

Then the massive beast made its way to the edge of the boat where Keiko stood and lifted its head out of the water.

I'd seen a makara before. When I was a vampire, my elf boyfriend (long story) took me makara watching. Think of it as whale watching for the divine. That day I saw dozens of makara, each one unique, each one half-terrestrial animal, half-leviathan. Elephant heads, crocodile heads, zebra heads ...

But despite seeing so many, I never saw one with an eagle's head. Except this one's head wasn't exactly an eagle. Sure, it had the golden beak and white feathers, but it also had elf-like ears. It was a—

"A griffin," Jean said, snapping his fingers as he came to the same conclusion as me. "This guy is half-griffin and he just fought off a bunch of meres." He snapped his fingers twice more before bursting out into laughter. "Meres Griffin! That's hilarious."

"Not a mere ... he's a makara."

"I know," Jean said waving a dismissive hand, "but he's in the water and ... come on! Meres Griffin! That's comedy gold."

I had to admit that was a pretty funny pop reference. Then I looked over at Keiko who continued to give him a blank stare. "Dare da?"

"Meres Griffin ... like Merv Griffin. You know, the sweepstakes guy," Jean said.

More blank looks.

"He was the Regis Philban of the 1960s," I added.

Her blank look got blanker.

"Ryan Seacrest. He was the Ryan Seacrest of the 1960s," Jean said, then turning to me, "Get with the times."

"Ahh, American Idol. Wakata," Keiko said with a nod of recognition before adding, *"Ukeru janai."*

"Agreed," I said. "You aren't as funny as you think."

"Sure I am," he muttered to himself, hurt. "Wait until I tell Bella. She's going to keel over laughing."

21

HIKING THROUGH THE JUNGLE
IS FIVE STAR ENOUGH FOR ME

*W*e threw Meres Griffin (as Jean insisted on calling him) a rope and the giant makara pulled us to Kakusareta Taiyo island. Given how far we had left to go, the makara was surprisingly fast. I mean faster-than-working-engines fast, and we got to the island before dawn.

Once there, Keiko whispered something to the makara. It nodded its griffin head before diving into the deep. The noro priestess bowed and turned to us. "The makara—"

"Meres Griffin," Jean corrected.

"*Urasai,*" Keiko spat before continuing. "The makara agrees to wait for our return. He will ensure we get back to the mainland safely." She turned to Jean. "He makes no such guarantee for you."

"Oh yes he does," Jean said as he unpacked an inflatable rowboat, dropping it in the water just after pulling the cord. The thing fully inflated before hitting the surface. "He loves his new name and loves me for giving it to him."

"Sure he does," I said, and hoisted myself over the edge and into the floating balloon. "After all, who doesn't love pun-based nicknames?"

↔

We paddled to shore, where a crisp beach waited for us. It was the kind of place dreams were made of, with raw, sienna-colored sand that no human foot seemed to have trounced on until now.

"Holy wow. Bella would love this place," Jean murmured under his breath, evidently just as impressed as I was.

Keiko surveyed the land with an approving nod. "The gods are gone, but they have not taken all of their divinity with them."

"True that," Jean said.

"True that," I agreed, pulling back my sleeve and looking at my map.

Now that we were on the island, it morphed, the ebbing blue and orange lines now showing the outskirts of the island we were on like we had just zoomed in on Google Maps. But even though it now only showed the island, it showed the *whole* island.

We were closer, but still not close enough to know exactly where we were.

I wondered if we just wandered about, whether we'd eventually hit a spot where the map would zoom in even more.

Jean looked at my arm. "Cute freckles."

"I'm not looking at my freckles, jerk."

"I know," he said. "You're looking at your invisible map. What's it telling you?"

"That you're an ass."

"Not a very impressive map if it can only state the obvious," he said without missing a beat.

I groaned, but couldn't help cracking a smile. "You're not funny."

"I am," he said, walking ahead of us. "And before we part ways, I'm going to have you keeled over in laughter."

"Mukatsuku," Keiko said after him, her face distorted by her disdain.

"Amen to that, sister," I agreed.

. . .

↔

As much as we all would have loved to stay on that secluded, perfect beach for the rest of our lives, we had a museum to find. I lugged the backpack Jean had given me up the beach toward the tree line, wondering how many stone guardians, yokai and other nasties waited for us in there.

From the way Jean carried his shotgun, I deduced that he wondered the same. Keiko, on the other hand, didn't even bother pulling out her telescopic baton.

After all, this was her island. Or at least, the island that housed the community she'd grown up in.

Breaking through the tree line, Jean looked at his Mickey Mouse watch and started singing "Swing on a Star" by Bing Crosby. He got to the first verse before saying, "No magic," then gestured for us to take the lead, presumably so he could watch our backs (and because he gave me a wee bit of a pervy vibe, to also *watch* our backs).

Keiko marched into the brush and I had to walk at double speed to catch up. Once I was next to her, matching her speed, I said, "You didn't need to come." I had meant to say it as a way of thanks, but me being socially awkward, not-entirely-in-touch-with-my-feelings me, it came off more as an admonishment than anything else.

Keiko took several steps before acknowledging me, her expression one of deep thought, like she was wrestling with telling me something. "I did," she finally said. "I owe you a great debt for what you did for my grandmother."

Bullshit, I thought. I'd spent years studying, hunting and terrorizing humans, and in that time, I'd seen it all. The nervous tics, the unconscious gestures that betray a lie or a bluff. The subtle things the body says even when your lips say something else.

And just because Keiko was a young, beautiful noro didn't mean she didn't have some of the telltale signs of a lie. Hers was holding in her breath a fraction of a second too long before speaking. That, and the fact that she hadn't looked at me since we landed on this island, told me she wasn't here just because of some ancient family debt.

She was here for reasons of her own.

I considered calling her out, telling her to fess up, but instead I decided to let it go. *Besides*, I thought, *it's not like I can force her to tell me the truth*.

"I am telling the truth," she said, annoyance in her voice. "I am here to repay our debt to you."

"Shoot," I said. "You weren't meant to hear that."

"Then why did you say it?" she asked, obviously unfamiliar with my eccentric (and terribly cute, right?) habit of thinking out loud.

"Ahh, I didn't mean to," I said.

"But you said—"

"What I mean is that I didn't mean to say that you weren't telling the truth. I meant that you aren't telling me the *whole* truth." If I was already in a hole, might as well keep digging.

She paused, held in her breath for that fraction of a second too long, and said, "It was my grandmother's greatest wish that she meet you once again. I'm here to make sure that you live long enough to see my grandmother before she dies. But if it is the truth you want … I am not here because I like you. In the few hours I have known you, I have been attacked, my car destroyed, then arrested and finally coerced into giving the U.S. military access to one of the gods' greatest secrets."

"Got it," I said. "Now we're starting to get somewhere. Still not the whole truth, but at least you're giving me more of it—"

"*Mukatsuku*," she spat. "Who are you to know my truths?"

I couldn't tell if she meant that like "who are you to know if I am telling the truth?" or that I was unworthy of her truths. Either way, she'd just admitted that she was holding back on me.

"I'm just an ex-vamp trying to make amends for hundreds of years of death," I said in my best Julia Roberts *Knotting Hill* voice. *I'm just a girl …*

But Keiko either didn't like that movie, or she wasn't in the mood.

"There is only one way I know of to make amends for the horrors inflicted by one such as you," she said. "Seppukura."

That got me to stop marching. She took on ahead, not slowing down just because I had.

I watched the noro speed ahead. *So, not a Julia Roberts fan*, I thought. And that had gotten serious real fast; she'd just asked me to kill myself. And not in a fun, playful, bantering way. She meant the full-on ritualistic, very painful way. But she'd told me to kill myself.

In Japanese culture, especially Okinawan, the worst thing you can say to someone is, *"Kurosi tai."* I want to kill you. It is the equivalent of using the s-word combined with the f- and c-words and the just-about-every-other-letter-in-the-alphabet word.

So it wasn't something Keiko said lightly.

And as ubiquitous as seppukura was in Japanese culture, it wasn't part of Ryukyu culture, and it wasn't something a noro would ever advocate.

For someone like Keiko to suggest that meant one of two things: she really didn't want me to hand over the keys to the museum to Jean, or she wasn't who she claimed to be.

I thought back to the Okinawan guards who had refused to train their guns on her and how she was able to summon the makaru Meres Griffin ... not something a normal human could do, so her *not* being a noro was out.

Which meant that she was here to stop us from getting to the museum (I was getting sick of referring to it as the God's Museum of Everything). If that was the case, how far was she willing to go and did we just invite a cute and very capable assassin on our little jaunt?

I shook my head. I had to be wrong about her. If she didn't want us to find the museum, then why get us so close? Why stop the meres from killing us? Why volunteer to help in the first place?

Yeah, I thought (making sure my mouth was closed), *I'm probably wrong about Keiko and she isn't some priestess with a plan.*

↔

We walked in silence for many hours, Keiko marching ahead without looking at a map or stopping to get her bearings through some other method like a compass, gauging where the sun was or listening for a stream.

She just marched and I was beginning to think she was trying to commit murder by hiking. Jean was apparently thinking the same thing, because he asked several times if we were there yet like a six-year-old does to annoy his parents.

Keiko ignored him, keeping her steady march through the thick tropical forest. And even though we weren't following a path, I noted that she somehow managed to navigate the forest without ever having to double back or cut down any plants to make space to get through. She always managed to find terrain just tame enough for us to walk without really slowing us down.

It was starting to get dark when Jean's comments went from, "Are we there yet?" to a more serious, "Let's set up camp before it gets dark." Although I agreed with him, I didn't say anything lest she suggest I climb the highest tree I could find and jump off.

Jean was losing patience and I could hear him starting to pick up the pace, presumably to catch up with Keiko and stop her maniacal march, when she suddenly broke through the tree line and stopped.

We caught up and breaking through the tree line myself, I saw the very last thing I expected. It was a sight that I would forever remember as one of the most startling, bewildering things I'd ever encountered.

A hotel that was in the middle of nowhere.

22

HOTEL CASTLES FOR THE RICH AND DEAD

*T*he forest abruptly ended, revealing an open field with stone gardens that wove from the forest line and up a hill toward what must have been an old, Edo-period Japanese castle.

I felt like I had been transported back in time to sixteenth-century Japan. And I would have kept that feeling if it wasn't for a giant aluminum structure standing next to the building with the Kanji symbols for "water" and "tower" inscribed under a very modern-looking logo.

We walked toward the castle, weaving our way through the stone zen garden where two giant, spider-like creatures called jorogumo used their spiked legs to rake the stones with expert care. I'd seen a jorogumo before: they were incredibly fast, using their eight legs to hop about with the same agility and grace as their insect-sized counterparts. But here, tending to this garden, their actions were deliberate, slow. Meditative.

Mulling about on the pathways between the gardens were several yokai. I saw a kitsune with its nine fox tails lounging on a bench, a shirime who was thankfully sitting on his butt, thus not exposing the eye he had in the place used by most of us during our daily ablutions, a rokurokubi who bowed at us as we passed, her giraffe-like neck towering over an otherwise normal-looking female body, and a tengu practicing tai chi in the distance, his red, taloned feet moving with a grace I've rarely seen.

There were even two futakuchi-onnas walking hand in hand.

I quickly counted the yokai and, turning to Jean, said, "You see sixteen of them, right?" I was concerned that some of them might be the attacking ghosts from earlier.

Jean shook his head. "Seventeen." He pointed at a stack of smooth, white rocks where a thunderbird from Native American tradition sat.

"Ahh," I said, annoyed with myself for missing that one, but doubly annoyed that Jean had seen it when I hadn't. I'm not competitive. Really, I'm not.

The thunderbird followed our progression through the garden with a calm, watchful eye. Normally thunderbirds were wild beasts covered in crackling, electric energy, but the only electricity this one exuded was a light current that jumped between its peaceful eyes.

Whatever this place was, it possessed a serene quality pervasive enough to tame one of the most volatile creatures in all creation.

As soon as we walked over the hill and beyond the yokai and stone gardens, we saw the hotel, which from the outside looked like an old Japanese castle. Wooden, sloping roofs, clay shingles, arches ... I felt like I was in a scene from *Ninja Scroll*.

I would have mistaken it for an actual castle except for the kanji and hiragana (two of the three Japanese alphabets commonly used) sign that sat just above its copper-colored doors. It read *The Celestial Solace Hotel.*

We walked up the middle path toward the entrance and as we made our way, the yokai all bowed in our direction.

And by "our," I mean in Keiko's direction. We were more of a suspicious afterthought.

↔

We walked to the massive entrance, where two giant knockers waited for us. Keiko pulled one of them twice, paused for a second, then knocked it a third time.

The door clicked open and a giant nuppeppo appeared. Think animated lumps of human flesh, but don't get these guys confused with the blob (a real creature, by the way). The blob had no control over its mass, rolling about and consuming everything in its path. The nuppeppo, on the other hand, was a creature that, although it looked like a ball of flesh-colored Play-Doh, had full control of itself.

This one had two stumpy legs that it shuffled about with and when it opened the door, it had created a little hand for itself that it contracted when it saw us.

But despite the short legs, this thing had shaped itself tall. Which made sense: the doors were huge, and the knocker that Keiko had just pulled not even really human-sized.

The nuppeppo looked down at us with two dimples that sat somewhere in the top of its mass before the flesh in its middle split apart, making a tearing sound (what ripping a piece of flesh-like paper would sound like), creating what I assumed was its mouth.

A mouth that smiled.

Then spoke.

"Keiko-sama," it said, *"hisashiburi."* The flesh morphed into something that vaguely resembled a human body that bowed, before turning into a shape that reminded me of a giant muffin.

"Masamitsu-san. Yes, indeed it has been a long time," Keiko said in English, obviously for our benefit.

"Tomodachi-da?" Masamitsu's mass asked.

"Yes," Keiko said, "my friends."

The mass's skin ripped again (sending chills up my spine), giving us another smile before letting us in. I wondered what it would have done to us if Keiko hadn't given us her "friendship" seal of approval.

↔

. . .

The inside was just as lavish as the outside, with marble flooring that led to a molasses-colored desk in immaculate condition. We walked by two shoulder-height vases that I immediately recognized to be from the Ming dynasty.

In the center of the room hung a magnificent chandelier that looked like frozen lightning, each electric tip piercing into a diamond of light. "They're real stars," Keiko said, following my gaze.

"No way."

"*Honto ni,*" Keiko said. "Real stars. They are from the collection of the BisMark, an Other of great power. He bequeathed the chandelier to this hotel before the continents separated."

"Wow," I said, staring up as we passed under it, "talk about capturing lightning in a bottle."

This place was magnificent, with every decorative item being older than most pyramids. On the walls hung several tapestries depicting various scenes, one of which reminded me of— "Hold on a second," I said pointing at the center tapestry. "That's not one of Katsushika Hokusai's paintings, is it?"

Keiko gave me an appreciative smile. "Indeed. Katsushika Hokusai was a friend of the Celestial Solace Hotel. Before he died, that is."

"You're messing with me."

"No mess, just awe," she said, pointing to the front desk where a tanuki sat on his, well, on his beanbag reading a newspaper. Tanuki looked like raccoons except that their ... ahem, family jewels were the size of a gazebo. They used their assets in battle, as a defense mechanism and, seeing him now, as a seat.

"Aki-sama," Keiko said with a deep bow.

The tanuki looked up from his newspaper and, removing his reading glasses, gave Keiko a fang-filled smile. He looked at us and seeing us as *gaijin*, spoke in English. "Keiko-sama, you honor us with your presence." He folded the paper, looking at its date before saying, "We did not expect a noro to grace us with her presence until then. Are you here to attend tonight's New Year's party?"

But from the way the tanuki spoke, I knew that the raccoon-like creature already knew the answer to his question. Back in the day, the tanuki were divine judges, often ruling over disputes between gods, let alone Others. They were some of the most respected creatures in all of creation, despite their vulgar appearance.

Looking at the creature now, part of me wondered if their incredible balls (argh, I hated that word) helped them when dealing with bitchy gods. I mean, they could literally throw their weight around and ... well, you get the idea.

Keiko shook her head. "I fear that our presence is for other, less festive reasons, and I ask permission to stay here one night while continuing our quest."

Aki eyed us both carefully. "These two have much blood on their hands, Keiko-san."

"I know."

"And much of that blood was taken for ill purposes."

"I know," the noro repeated.

"But not all of it. Much was taken to protect others."

Keiko nodded. I was starting to understand what was happening here. He was judging us. If we passed, we got to stay. If we failed ... I wasn't sure what happened then.

"If I may ..." I started, but before I could say another word the tanuki shot me a look of such authority that I froze in place. I was so stunned by his gaze that I thought he must have burned time to have such an effect.

But he hadn't; it was just who he was. A creature that demanded respect.

I diverted my gaze, but I could still feel him looking at me. "Blood stains them both, for good and ill. But their deeds are in balance. They may stay," he said to Keiko.

As he spoke those words, I noted the tension in Keiko's body, her fists balling up as if she was angered by Aki's decision. What was going on here?

The tanuki handed over three keys to Keiko before turning to Jean and me. "*Gai-koko-jin*, please understand that this place is a sanctuary. Under no circumstances will I tolerate violence of any kind."

"Understood," I said.

Jean, on the other hand, shook his head. "You mean *physical* violence. I mean, Mr Tanuki, Judge, Sir … I've got this problem with my mouth and I'm not sure I can play nice for a whole night—"

"Of any kind."

"OK, so live by Thumper's rule."

All three of us gave Jean a curious look.

"You know: if you don't have anything nice to say, don't say anything at all," he clarified.

"Oh, thank the GoneGods," I said in an exasperated tone. "You'll finally shut up."

Much to my relief, both Keiko and Aki chuckled. I leaned in so Jean could hear me. "Now that's how to be funny."

23

IT'S LIKE DISCOVERING THE
WORLD'S FLAT

*M*asamitsu escorted us to our rooms, three little hands popping out of his flesh to carry our bags. He was surprisingly spry for a blob and as we walked, I found myself wondering what his BMI was.

But that was a fleeting thought, especially with all the beauty surrounding me. When we came onto the second floor, we were greeted by the sound of a tinkling fountain that reminded me of a hollow tube being knocked softly on the edge of a surface.

I paused at a railing that overlooked a courtyard in the center of the hotel. Below me, another zen garden with a pond of yellow, white and black koi and the fountain that lay at the edge of it.

I almost wished we were staying for longer than a night.

And my room was no different with ancient Persian rugs, lamps that must have been made around the time glass was invented and a duvet that was so soft it was probably stuffed with angel feathers. If only Egya could see this ... then he'd know what true First Class looked like.

My mind jumped to Egya and Deirdre sitting in some cell while I was off trying to get my soul ... ahem, I mean, save the world. I needed to complete my mission and get them out of whatever hellhole they were in. Then again, knowing Deirdre, she was probably naked and driving the lonely soldiers crazy, each one of them falling over each other to win her favor. And as for Egya, he was probably the best thing these guys had since Bob Hope (the kid could hold court when he wanted to).

Shaking my head free from thoughts about them, I refocused on the task at hand and checked my map. It hadn't zoomed in any farther and I was beginning to wonder if we were in the right place. After all, who was to say that this place was the right place? Just because Kenji had heard a rumor didn't make that rumor correct.

For all I knew, we were on the wrong island. Hell, the wrong ocean. Who knew? I was beginning to think that Keiko knew something I didn't.

But whatever she knew, she wasn't sharing, so I'd just have to wait and see. I took a shower and was shocked at how amazing the water pressure was. Once done, I got dressed in a fresh pair of clothes that I found in the backpack. Sadly, the only clothes provided were green, camouflage army fatigues. Luckily there was also a pair of scissors and an emergency sewing kit. Using both and my impeccable sense of style, I cute-ified the outfit, making it less army and more ironic chic. The only part of my new outfit that I really struggled with were the sleeves. I was partly worried that more mokumokuren would show up and do their drone-hover-stare thing at my arm, but I was mostly worried about mosquitos. This island was teeming with them.

In the end, I went sleeveless. The sacrifices I made for fashion.

That done, I sat on the (extremely plush) bed, planning on chilling for a bit before going down.

Of course, chilling after hours of hiking turned into a nap that would have lasted through the New Year if it wasn't for an annoying man knocking on my door.

↔

"What?" I growled as I opened the door. Jean stood there in army fatigues that he wasn't wearing ironically. Still, his muscular frame filled the outfit and I fear that I was momentarily guilty of being one of those girls who likes a man in uniform.

Then he spoke, curing me of any potential lapses in judgement. "Cute," he said. "Not the direction I would have gone, but not bad considering."

"Ah, huh," I said.

He held out the crook of his arm. "Care to join me downstairs for the festivities?"

"Festivities?"

"Yeah, it's an hour before the new year and from what I've gathered, the party is thumping down there."

"Party?" I looked at my arm. The map hadn't changed.

"Still nothing?"

"Nothing. For all we know, we're nowhere close to the place."

"Then we have nothing to lose." He held out his elbow, extending it farther.

"Come on," he said when I didn't take it, "it's not like we're going anywhere tonight and we're in a 'no violence' zone, so we don't have to worry about watching our sixes for once. Plus, in case you haven't heard, there's a party down there. A party!" he did a little jig before offering his arm again.

I felt my stomach growl. "Party means food, right?"

Jean nodded.

"And where's Keiko?"

"I knocked on her door. No answer, which probably means she's downstairs."

"Fine," I said and took his arm.

↔

We went downstairs and were hardly halfway down when we saw one of the most diverse collections of Others I had ever seen in one place. There weren't just yokai and other Japanese Others—there were mystical creatures of all walks of life from diverse traditions.

This would have been a comforting place if it wasn't for what Kenji had said earlier: the Others were gathering for the Three Who Are One's arrival. And given that the Others who attacked the base flew under the same banner, I didn't think the Three Who Are One—whatever it was—was a good thing.

Masamitsu was waiting at the stairwell. As soon as we made it to the bottom step the nuppeppo animated, extending a hand that gestured for us to follow blob.

We did. As we weaved our way through the crowd, I saw several of the Others wearing the same hoop necklace I'd seen around the yeti's neck at the airport. There was even—

"Harry?" I said.

The yeti had ditched his Blue Jays bed sheet, going au naturel. "Kat?" he said affectionately, bending down to kiss my cheeks. "I had no idea you were a part of these circles." He gestured around him.

"Ex-vamp," I offered.

"Of course—I knew there was something special about you. So how are you enjoying the festivities so far?"

I gestured with a wavering, horizontal palm. "I'll enjoy it more when I get some food in my belly. It was quite the journey getting here."

"Tell me about it," the yeti said. "I had to burn seven hours of time to get to this place. Small price to pay for a night like this. I mean, look around. So many Others in one spot. I haven't attended a party like this since the wedding party that sank Atlantis five thousand years ago."

"You were ..." I started, but shook my head. There were more important things to focus on than pressing Harry for details about Atlantis. "That long," I finally muttered.

"That long," he repeated.

Jean whistled from across the room. "Kat," he said, pointing at an empty table, "come on."

"Your boyfriend is impatient."

"My boyfriend isn't even my friend. Just a travelling companion that helped me get here given I don't have any time to burn."

"Ahh, I see. Still, he looks like he really wants you to come over."

I sighed as I watched Jean continue to play his game of charades even though I'd gotten it seven seconds ago. "Yeah, I better go. If I don't see you before the countdown, Happy New Year, Harry."

"You too, Ms. Darling. You, too."

↔

I walked over to the tatami mat with a short table on it that Jean had staked out for us. There was already a plethora of food atop it that Jean had already ordered. I mentally gave him a point for ordering, which put him up to minus about a billion points.

Still, progress.

I sat on the mat and immediately started stuffing my mouth. To say I was hungry after our speed boat chase and our seemingly endless walk through the forest would be an understatement. Jean must have been as hungry as me, but was surprisingly more restrained, taking in his surroundings before sitting.

Eventually he sat down and poured me a sip of Habu Sake from the clay flask on the table. "So, many of these Others are here for the Celestial Solace because they believe in the Three Who Are One?"

So he had been thinking the same thing as me.

I shrugged.

"I guess it's a good thing we've got that 'no violence' thing in place, huh?" he said, waving at three wendigos who stared at us with hate-filled, fiery eyes which were all the more pronounced against their snow-white fur.

If my thermal temperature wasn't going up so fast from all the food I was putting in me, I might have shivered.

"Guess so," I said between bites of edamame and takoyaki.

"Look at this place. It's filled with all kinds of Others. I mean, look over there. It's a peri," he said.

"You mean those winged, fairy-like spirits from Persian mythology? You know, the ones that rank somewhere between angels and demons?"

"Very good," Jean said, impressed. "Let's try another one." He pointed at a little bearded man who was mostly a head on a pair of stick-thin legs.

"Easy," I said. "A puk-wudjie. Native American mythology. From somewhere in the Delaware region."

"Excellent. How about—"

"Nope, my turn." I scanned the room, looking for something that would really surprise him. I finally settled on a creature that looked like a pink dolphin standing on two legs.

Jean exaggerated a yawn. "Encantado. Amazon River, shapeshifter and a bit of player. They used to lure unsuspecting women back to their lairs to … you know, make whoopie."

"Seriously? 'Make whoopie?' That was cliché in the '60s. I should know—I was there."

We both chuckled before Jean shook his head as he continued scanning the room. "The question isn't *what* are they, but how did they all get here?" Jean said. "It's not like there's an Other TripAdvisor and—"

Before he could finish his thought, Aki rolled over on his massive testicles. "May I?" he asked. From the way he rolled in, I saw that he'd had a little too much sake already.

I bowed, gesturing for the tanuki to join us.

The raccoon creature parked his appendage next to the table, the rest of his body joining us on the mat. "How are you enjoying your stay?" Aki asked.

"This place is incredible," I said. "And the fact that you have electricity and hot water out here is …"

"Yes, it is good for this place to be full again. Since the gods left, we haven't had many patrons. But not tonight. Tonight, we are full." Aki lifted his sake with pride and joy before downing it and filling his tumbler once more. "Back before the gods left, this whole place was powered by magic. Now that they are gone, we've had to use more mundane methods. It took effort and the aid of several dwarves and ramidreju before we managed to install plumbing and electricity here. We even have Wi-Fi." He chuckled.

"Where are you pumping it in from?" Jean asked. "It's not like there's a power plant or underground piping to funnel water or—"

Aki shook his head. "There is. A small one that powers the noro community. It was installed after the war and the priestesses have been kind enough to let us use the infrastructure without alerting the authorities. They also called the Okinawan municipalities to build that tower, claiming this place as an extension of their village—another benefit we get for free because of their generosity. But the noro have always been kind to Others. Even after the gods left, they took in many of the more unique Others who struggled to adjust to mortal life."

"Humph," Jean said. "That may be, but how do you pay the non-noro help? Dwarves aren't cheap and ramidreju, well, they're downright criminals."

Aki gave Jean a curious look. "You are familiar with the ramidreju?" The tanuki was obviously surprised by Jean's knowledge.

So was I. I thought I knew my Others, but I'd never heard of the ramidreju before, and the fact that Jean had meant he'd won our little game. Not that I was going to give him the satisfaction; as soon as he turned his back, I'd jump on Wikipedia and look the damn diggers up.

" 'Familiar' is a strong word," Jean said. "I met a couple a year or so back when they were tunneling under Paradise Lot's downtown. The whole street nearly sank and I had to go down there and get them to stop."

"By killing them?" I asked.

"No," Jean said. "Not every solution needs a gun. I talked to them. They love mushrooms. Whitecaps, to be specific. We worked out a deal: they'd create subterranean housing for trolls, dwarves and other Others that like to live underground, and I made it so they'd get as many whitecaps as their shovel-like claws could handle. Ever try to pay a creature in mushrooms? We trucked in tons of fungi in from every distributor within three hundred miles."

"Intriguing, Mr. ..."

"Matthias. Jean-Luc Matthias."

"As in John, Luke, Matthew, only missing the Mark?"

"Yes. Ha-ha," he said sarcastically. "I haven't heard that one before. No seriously, you are the first person to say that to me."

Aki chuckled.

"Aki-sama," I said, "my sardonic friend here raised a good question before you graced us with your presence. How is it that so many Others know of this place?"

"Because we are famous."

"I never heard of you," I said.

"Amongst *Others*, we're famous," giving me a look that I'd gotten many times as a vampire. The one that said, 'You wouldn't understand ... you know, being a half-breed and all ...'

He must have sensed my annoyance, because he quickly added, "We have existed since the dawn of time."

I gathered he wasn't exaggerating when he said "dawn of time."

"We have hosted Others from all walks of life, for all kinds of celebrations. We were where the gods came when negotiating with the Laws of Nature."

"Laws?" I asked.

The tanuki nodded. "Yes. Time, gravity, death, to name a few. At one point or another, all the gods have spent time here. Both living and dead."

"Dead? As in dead gods?"

Again the raccoon-like creature nodded. "Even gods can die, but unlike the rest of us, they do not completely fade away. Their essence remains, like a light that cannot be extinguished. And when a god dies or is killed, it is tradition to host them here for their send-off."

"And where do dead gods get sent off to?" I asked.

"Usually some sarcophagus placed somewhere where they can't do any harm."

"Humph, I see," I said, looking around. "I do have another question. I don't mean to be rude or anything, but as lovely as this place is, how is it possible that so many have come here when …?" I didn't even know how to finish my question.

"When *here* is in the middle of nowhere?" Aki offered. "It is because this place wasn't always here. This hotel moved from domain to domain, both on the mortal and divine planes. These halls have been encased in the flames of Hades as well as the bowels of RE. Never static, never confined to one place and one time. Until, that is, the gods left and we were forced to find a home on Earth."

I shook my head. I'd never heard of such a place before, but I did know one thing about Others: there were rules. And as much as this hotel could move from place to place, that didn't mean they could chose anywhere they liked, all willy-nilly like.

"Why here?" I asked.

"Because this was the only plane of existence that remained."

"No, why *here*? Why this island?" I was remembering something the futakuchi-onna on the plane had said. At the time, it didn't make sense, but now it was all falling into place.

"The noro, they—" Aki began.

"Again, no. This place is not arbitrary. The hotel didn't choose this place just because. In fact, I don't think this hotel moves at all, does it?" I said, hitting myself in the head with the palm of my hand. Hard. "How could I have been so stupid and not seen the connection? It was staring me right in my face. The museum, this hotel, the Heralds of Three Who Are One and Harry's hoop necklace … they're all connected to the human new year and the Celestial Solace."

I flattened out a napkin and, using a chopstick as a pen and soy sauce as ink, drew the hotel in the center. "This point is here. This hotel. But there is a network around it. An invisible, shifting plane that rotates like the sun does around the Earth." I drew a ring with the hotel at the bottommost point. Then evenly spacing the circles, I drew another circle and wrote the name of another plane of existence on it.

Heaven, Hell, Hades, Yomi, Elysium, all the heavens and hells, and then … Earth.

"This place is a static point on a spinning wheel. As the wheel rotates, the hotel 'moves' into another plane of existence. Heaven"—I pointed at the circle labeled *Heaven*—"then the circle rotates, and now the hotel is in Hell." I pointed at the next point on my circle. "Right? That's how this works?"

The part I didn't say out loud was that I had an invisible map which only showed the outline of this island. It wasn't giving me any more specifics because there were no specifics to give. The museum wasn't even on this planet—yet. But come New Year's Day, the rotation would be complete. And for however long the rotation lasted, the museum would be on Earth.

Aki looked at my napkin, then me. "Yes," he said. "It is more complex than that simple circle, but yes. That is exactly how this works. Different domains find—well, *found*—their way to us, thus letting us overlap for a few days. By Earth's standards, of course. After all, eternity can be caught in a single second, can it not?" The tanuki looked at me, waiting for a reaction, but since I wasn't sure if he was being profound or making a joke, I just stared at him with a confused, blank expression.

Jean leaned in and whispered, "Clever girl."

↔

"When the gods left, the rotation—to use your analogy—ceased and the hotel found itself on Earth, on this island, at this time," Aki said.

"And what about the 'rotation?' Does it continue? Do the other planes continue to appear?"

The tanuki nodded. "It does, but every realm is closed and even though we may have entered the 'circle of Heaven' or 'Hell' or 'Nirvana,' the hotel does not move."

I was starting to understand better. Aki meant that, while the rotation still occurred, the hotel would not be possessed, for lack of a better word, by that realm any longer.

"But not all the realms are realms, are they? I mean, it's not just heavens and hells and purgatories, is it? There are other divine places not owned by a particular god or pantheon. Places that may have been shared by all of them, perhaps? For example, the museum."

The tanuki nodded again. "But such knowledge is dangerous. Especially in a godless world."

"Yomi … that's where those who follow Shinto go when they die. Well, went," I said. "And that domain is closed like everywhere else."

Aki took a long draw from his sake.

"Kenji told me that Yomi is also where the Kami Subete Hakubutsukan resides and because the rotation is going to align with that plane of existence, these Others believe it will actually appear." I stared hard at Aki. "But you don't, do you? I mean, if you did, you would never have opened this place up, would you?"

The tanuki nodded. "Just because you believe something is going to happen does not make it so. They are holding onto a past that will never be again."

"So they are waiting for the museum to come. Why? What are they hoping for?"

The tanuki nodded as if defeated. "The return of a god. Or I should say, the resurrection of three."

"But the gods are gone."

"Not all of them. Some remain."

"Bullshit," Jean said, his voice both harsh and quivering.

I understood where his anger and confusion came from; many humans didn't believe in God or the gods to begin with, and to be presented with undeniable proof they existed was hard enough. But to have that proof coupled with their abrupt and unexplained departure was a whole new level of existential fuck-uppedness.

Most of us spent years coming to terms with their existence, disappearance and the impending consequences of both. And now this drunk tanuki was telling us that all the gods *weren't* gone. That at least one of them still remained. Well, that wasn't something easy to accept.

"Like who?" I asked, my voice trembling.

"Not one," Aki said. He lifted three fur-covered fingers. "Three dead gods remain. And they hope that these gods shall live once more."

24

10, 9, 8 ... REALLY? THIS COULDN'T HAVE WAITED UNTIL NEW YEAR'S?

"Hold on," I said, "I thought you said that the dead gods were usually shuffled off to some sarcophagus where they couldn't do any more harm?"

"And where do you think those sarcophaguses are kept?" the drunk tanuki said, pouring himself one that was already one too many three drinks ago.

"In the museum," I said.

The tanuki gave me a thumbs-up. "You can't really kill a god, just weaken them and lock them away. And that is exactly what the Shinto gods did to Izanami-no-Mikoto, believing her decaying mind and body would destroy all life. As did the Norse gods believe when Baldr died. You see, not everyone cried for his death and, well, there was little motivation to resurrect him. But it was more than that for the Norse pantheon. They believed that a dead god was a sign of Ragnarok and rather than mess with fate and bring him back, they locked him away.

"Then there was Quetzalcoatl. He was the worst of the lot. Well, I say 'he,' but the truth was, 'he' was a bunch of birds. Seems that when he died his essence became a flock of birds of all sorts and, well, it's strange referring to hundreds of birds as a single being, but what can you do? I mean … gods, right? Anyway, the Aztec gods—who were no prizes of virtue, mercy or kindness themselves—chose to lock Quetzalcoatl away in the Kami Subete Hakubutsukan, thus ridding the world of a god they believed would ultimately lead to the end of all."

"Ever watch *Sesame Street?*" Jean asked.

"Excuse me?"

"You know: *three of these things belong together …*" he sang the tune from the old 1970's show. *"Three of these things are kind of the same …"*

"Yeah," I said, snapping my fingers as it dawned on me, too. "Three dead gods who were so despicable that the living gods locked them away rather than return them to life. But that's not all. They all were seen as signs or milestones in the apocalypse. Baldr was a sign of Ragnarok, Izanami was to infect all and Quetzalcoatl would lead to the end of all."

"Three Who Are One." Jean pointed to the crowd of Others who were obviously for resurrecting the gods. "They're not here to usher in gods so that they can return to the old system. They're trying to usher in the apocalypse."

"And Ragnarok," I added.

"And Ragnarok," Jean agreed. "Why is it always Ragnarok?"

"Chris Hemsworth fans?" I offered.

"Yeah, but why can't they be obsessed with his role in the *Ghostbusters* reboot?"

I chuckled at Jean's gallows humor before the seriousness of the situation returned to me. "So do you think that they're right? That these gods are coming back?"

The tanuki shrugged. "When I condemned Quetzalcoatl to continued death, I did so knowing that of every case I had ever presided over, this was my most important one, for I had just locked away a great evil." He sighed, downing another sake. "I know what I hope will happen: nothing. That with the gods' departure and the resulting limitations in magic, I pray that this sphere of existence will pass through us and we will feel like … like a ghost is gliding through us."

"That's your hope. What's your fear?" Jean asked.

"That Yomi opens and these idiots somehow resurrect the dead gods."

"Yep, that sums it up for me," Jean said.

The tanuki lifted a skinny black finger. "Not done. For my fear continues down the dark, dark path of war led by power-hungry gods that will result in the apocalypse promised by Revelations, Ragnarok and the End of Days, instead of the one we actually got which—all things considered—wasn't really that bad. I mean, we still have sake." He let out a chortle as he threw away his cup and started drinking directly from the bottle.

I thought about the dead gods being locked away in the museum. It was the perfect solution for dealing with volatile things like dead, evil gods and items of intense magical properties. Keep the dangerous magic out of any realm it could hurt without completely severing the ties. Like having an offshore nuclear power plant.

And that nuclear power plant not only had my soul, but it also contained three dead gods who were trying to resurrect themselves. And that, I realized, was why my soul hadn't come back to me.

The dead gods had stopped my soul from returning. They were going to use it to try to raise themselves.

And *that* (remarkably) wasn't even the worst of it.

The thing that really worried me was the attacking Others who were gathering just because they hoped the gods would come back. Well, three of them would come back to life, that was. They were so desperate that the thought of a god's return—even an asshole of a god —was enough of a rally to get them to gather in force.

I didn't know what was worse: the three dead gods actually being resurrected and all-out war, or nothing happening and those Others that had pinned their hopes on a fairytale coming true starting an all-out war out of sheer despair. Suicide by fighting.

My head spun in anticipation as every fiber of my being worried about the terrible outcome that would come to pass no matter what. With or without my soul.

My soul ... that's why I was here. That's how I'd found myself in the middle of all this. I couldn't deny that I wanted it back. I needed it back if I was going to banish this emptiness inside me and find joy once again.

War was coming, and if I was going to face the it, then let it be with all of me intact.

Of course, all those thoughts would be meaningless if New Year's came and nothing happened.

I looked at my arm and saw the morphing blues and oranges swirling on my skin, and all they showed was this island and nothing else.

I tapped my wrist at Jean. He turned the Mickey Mouse face in my direction; a couple more minutes until New Year's. A couple minutes that felt like an eternity.

Staring at the crowd of Others, I counted the seconds as if I could push time forward through sheer will.

An impossibly long minute passed. Then another. Until finally the fated countdown began.

10 ...

9 ...

8 ...

I saw three oni demons draw close to the two wendigos in the corner. They were clearly gathering to prepare for whatever came next.

7 ...

6 ...

5 ...

Harry lifted a glass in my direction. He wasn't a believer, nor a Herald of the Three Who Are One. He was just a yeti trying to recapture some of the joy lost when the gods left. For him, if not myself, I prayed nothing would happen.

4 ...

3 ...

And as for myself, I prayed for an impossible miracle. One where my soul somehow found its way back to me. One where the warring Others retreated and the humans didn't pursue. One where peace would prevail. And if not peace, then common sense and decency.

2 …

But common sense and decency were in short supply these days. As for miracles? The gods hadn't left any behind when they went away.

1 …

Normally there's an eruption of joy at the fated final second. But not that New Year's and not in the Celestial Solace Hotel. The room went dead silent as everyone held their breath in anticipation of something, anything happening.

Nothing happened … until, that was, everything did.

First the Earth shook as a trumpet heralded impending doom. And as I covered my ears in pain, I watched in horror as the ground opened up, causing the Others who had been on the dance floor to fall within its blackened gulf.

"What's happening?" I asked Aki.

The tanuki shook his head as his eyes widened in shock and fear. "When the celestial path would come upon us, this place would be consumed by that reality. But with the magic gone, it seems that the new reality is trying to consume this one."

Oh good, I thought.

End of Part 3

PART IV
INTERMISSION

25

OKINAWA — WORLD WAR II

ecades Ago —

Smoke rose from the chimney in billows of black and gray. They were burning wet wood, which was strange not only because it was the middle of summer, but the thick smoldering clouds would tell everyone within a few miles exactly where they were.

Still, there was life inside. We approached the old stone house cautiously, our hands raised in the air as we spoke very loudly so as to not scare whoever was inside. Not that we had much of a chance of doing that; I was a *gaijin* with amber hair, walking in the middle of the night.

That's why I kept Blue behind me. Just in case whoever was a soldier or someone who had managed to get their hands on a gun. But the person who came outside wasn't a soldier and the only thing she held in her hands were two bowls of soup.

I should have known right then and there we were in trouble, but even vampires get tired and when I saw Blue's eyes light up with the prospect of eating hot food for a change, I acquiesced and we walked inside.

↔

The home was completely stripped, every shred of furniture gone. Even the tatami mats had been ripped from the ground. But there were four walls and the windows were still intact enough to keep most of the chill out. The fire place was roaring and I understood what was happening: the friendly woman had been using the ripped-up tatami mats as kindling.

She gestured for us to sit, still not saying anything as she placed two bowls of soup before us. I didn't eat human food then, and given how hungry I was, it took every ounce of willpower to stop myself from eating the woman.

Well, every ounce of my willpower is a lie. The truth was, all I needed to do was see Blue's eagerness to stop myself.

The woman, who must have been in her mid-forties, gestured for me to eat. I politely declined, offering my bowl to Blue. The little girl took it greedily, pouring it into her nearly empty bowl and spooning away, loudly slurping with abandon.

Seeing that I wouldn't eat, the lady frowned and immediately grabbed my now empty bowl and filled it up. I looked at the steaming soup in dismay. The thing about food and vampires: we can eat it, we just don't like it. To us it tastes flat, flavorless. We could eat a meal prepared by a chef at a Michelin 3-star restaurant and it would still taste like cardboard.

The woman, without speaking, gestured at my bowl as though to push it toward me.

Blue silently pleaded with her eyes for me not to be rude. So I ate a few spoonfuls before putting the bowl down. This seemed to satisfy our hostess, who snarfed down her bowl before pouring herself another.

I watched as the two ate without speaking, their concentration on the food before them. When they were done, Blue said, *"Sugoyu ne!"* and stretched out to sleep.

The woman chuckled at this and, leaning against the wall, closed her eyes and started humming to herself.

So that was what this night was going to be. Two full humans—neither of whom I could eat—sleeping the wee hours away.

I thought about going on a hunt myself but decided to wait until I was sure they were both asleep. I'd also douse the fire before I left; I didn't want anyone stumbling upon this place while I wasn't around to protect Blue.

I stood up and was looking for something to safely put out the fire when I saw a small vial by the metal pot. The vial was brown in shape and stood about three inches high. There was no label, but there didn't need to be one—I knew exactly what it was.

I grabbed the woman, lifting her by the neck. "What did you do?" I screamed in Japanese.

The woman was already drifting off, her voice distant and slurred. "They all went to sleep, and so will we. Sleep now. Sleep forever."

"Kuso," I spat. I dropped the woman and went to Blue. She was out, which meant that enough of the poison had seeped into her body to knock her unconscious.

I sat her up and stuck two fingers in her throat, trying to force her to vomit. The little girl did, but from the mess that came out of her, I knew I was already too late.

Blue was going to die if I didn't do something to save her.

↔

Scooping up the fragile child in my arms, I cursed myself for being so careless. I was a monster of the night who had used a smile and the promise of safety to lure in my victims. And here we were in the middle of a war … I should have known we were in danger when I saw that smile.

I ran using every ounce of my vampiric speed and strength. But because I'd eaten some of that infernal food, I wasn't at full strength. I doubted I had eaten enough to kill me, but I'd had just enough to knock me out. I desperately wanted to sleep.

But I couldn't let myself do that; I needed to help Blue. So I was headed to the only place I could think of … Naha. I figured the island's capital would be the best place to find human life.

Humans we found, but life, that was harder to come by.

The city was all but abandoned, with a few stragglers who ran away as soon as they saw me. There were no soldiers mulling about, no Okinawans to be seen. Nothing and no one.

Just an empty city.

"Blue," I said, sitting her up. "Come on, Blue. Fight this." But the child didn't stir, her slumber well past that of sleep. She'd fallen into a coma and I knew that even if I found a doctor in a fully functioning ER ward, the chances of her making it through the night were nothing.

It seemed that my only options were try to turn her or let her die.

Either way, Blue was going to die.

I popped out my fangs and clamped them over her neck. All I needed to do was apply a little pressure. Not much—my fangs were razor sharp and her neck was soft, almost paper-thin.

But I didn't bite down on her. I didn't because I was selfish. I knew that once I'd turned her, the demon would take over and change who she was. She'd lose her soul … And the little girl I loved would be lost forever.

I pulled away and retracted my fangs. The sun would rise in a few hours and that was exactly how much time I estimated she had. *Ironic that a human girl should die with the coming light*, I thought, my head swimming with utter exhaustion as I lost all hope of saving her.

I stared down at the motionless body of the only human I had ever cared for in my three hundred years as a vampire. I loved her. That much was undeniable. She had reminded me what it felt like to be human. Tempered the beast, so to speak, and the human part of me that now dominated my very being didn't want her to die.

Worse, because I knew that with her death, the beast would come back stronger than ever. I would shut off any emotions resurrected by Blue. And the thought of losing the little bit of humanity I had left terrified me.

I thought of my father and how noble he was when he chose death over being consumed by the vampire virus. How he faced the dawn with a smile on his face and how, even though I had turned him hours earlier, he died a human.

That was when I realized I had one more option before me. Blue was going to die, but she didn't need to go alone. When the dawn came, I could go with her.

26

THE ONE AND ONLY CHAPTER LEFT

resent Day —

I've read it in books, seen it in movies, and every time I come across the phrase, "The earth opened up and swallowed [insert character's name here] whole," I roll my eyes. To me it's kind of like reading, "It was a dark and stormy night ..."

So when I say that the earth opened up and swallowed us whole, know that I don't use those words lightly. And if there was any other way to describe it, I would, but hey—some lines are classics for a reason.

The earth opened up, rumbling as if the very fabric of reality had torn open with a ripping clamor that was partly the sound of tearing cloth and partly the sound a thousand bass drums thumping all at once.

It reminded me of a STOMP concert.

The earth continued ripping open until the entire foyer of the hotel was gone. And then it just stopped. There was no warning, no indication that this was going to cease ... nothing but the absence of destruction.

Talk about anti-climactic.

Aki appraised the hole. "Interesting. That's never happened before."

"What?" I said, gazing over the edge. All I saw was a bottomless void with a few of the flying Others flapping their way up out of it. The other, wing-challenged Others didn't seem to fare as well and were probably splats Wile E. Coyote style at the bottom of this thing (that is, if there was a bottom).

The tanuki shook his head, the sway of it unhinged in that way only severely drunk people seem to manage. "The hole. Usually the hotel collapses into itself as it leaves one reality and enters another." He made a sucking noise. "And we've never had any guests actually die in the process."

Not sure what to say back, I turned and saw that the strong and brave Jean had disappeared (sarcasm, moi? Never!), leaving me alone in the room to assess my next move.

Looking up from the giant, gaping hole in the floor, I noticed that there were several mokumokuren all droning about staring at everything. At first I thought they were invisible to everyone but me, like they had been on the airplane and at the izakaya, but when Jean said, "Floating eyeballs ... yuck!" I realized that if he could see them, then others could also see them.

And what's more, what else was now *visible?*

My worst fear, coupled with heart-wrenching regret for my sleeveless fashion choice, was confirmed when a wendigo shouted, "She has the map to the Museum of Everything. Rip her arm from her body and let it lead us to glory!"

↔

The wendigo hadn't finished shouting the words when he leapt at me with his claws ready to tear my arm from my body. But before he could get to me Harry stepped in, giving the giant beast a swift round-house kick that sent him flying into the hole.

"How rude," Harry said. "We yetis are oft confused with those wendigos and I don't like it."

"Like Canadians being called Americans?" I offered.

"Exactly like that," he said, lifting his fists up in the manner of a nineteenth-century boxer. "Now if you don't mind making a run for it, I shall do my best to buy you some time." He let out a right hook that flattened a gorgon to what remained of the floor.

"Thanks," I said, and did what any hero would do when facing dozens of powerful adversaries.

I ran.

↔

I wasn't sure where to go. I was in the middle of an unfamiliar jungle, in a hotel that didn't exactly have fire exits, being chased by dozens of fanatical Others who wanted to rip my arm off.

Given my options, I figured the jungle was my best bet, but the only way outside that I knew of was through the front door and that was currently blocked.

I also knew that, as strong as Harry was, he'd only be able to keep this up for so long. I couldn't let him take a beating for me and since these guys wanted my arm and weren't playing nicely, I was going to have to take it away.

I ran up to the first landing of the stairwell, punching two hobgoblins in my way and climbing onto the bannister's edge. Lifting up my arm for everyone to see my vacillating tattoo, I screamed, "You want it? Come and get it," before leaping onto the chandelier hanging above the hole.

I underestimated the distance to the chandelier and nearly missed it, managing to catch a star (quite literally) that hung at the very outer edge. There was a collective gasp as I pulled myself onto one of the arms of the damn thing and hoisted myself up.

All thanks to the McGill Fitness Centre for the sheer power of those guns.

The room was silent, and turning to the mass of Others, I yelled, "Enough! This is crazy. All this for what? Some god that may or may not be down that hole? I know many of you want this," I said, showing them my arm. The arrow pointed down the hole. "And I know you think salvation is down there. But it's not. At best, there is nothing down there. At worst, there is a dead god who, if freed, will only enslave us. Is that what you want? Haven't we evolved beyond the need for a deity to tell us how to act, who to be?"

There was a hush, and for a second I thought that my riveting speech had won the hearts and minds of the Heralds.

All it had really won me was a few seconds of quiet. A skinwalker stood up and said, "Only gods can return our magic."

"Our immortality," said another.

"At what cost?" yelled a third, evidently on my side.

"Who cares about the cost? Anything is better than living with the humans."

"Hey!" I said. "I'm human."

"A human with the map."

"A human with the key."

"A human who's going to take a swan dive into that hole if you all don't calm the f—"

"Get her," screamed a jorogumo just before it shot a line of webbing at me.

The sticky thread wrapped around my wrist. The jorogumo bit it off and started pulling with its four arms. I had to use every ounce of my strength to hold onto the chandelier to stop myself from being pulled off.

I was losing this bizarre tug-of-war when a plate went flying at the jorogumo, hitting it square in its pincer-like nose and causing it to drop it webbing. "Leave the human alone," Harry said, staring down the creature. But in his distraction a cyclops managed to sneak behind the yeti and hit him over the head with a vase that was older than most mountains. The yeti took the blow with a shake of his head before grabbing the offending cyclops and poking him in the eye.

The one-eyed creature went down with a yelp. But you know what they say: when one cyclops goes down, one tanuki gets up.

OK, no one says that, but after what I saw, they really should start. Aki, seeing his precious vase destroyed, got up, swaying like a drunk on the deck of a boat on troubled waters and yelled, "I said ... no ... violence!"

Leaping off his own testicles, he spun with such speed and force that his appendage swung like a wrecking ball, knocking down several Others unfortunate enough to be nearby.

Talk about throwing your weight around.

As impressive as Aki was, not everyone's attention was on him. That became obvious when three banshees started shrieking while they grabbed everything that wasn't nailed down and started chucking it at me.

"Hey," I said, "I thought that you guys wanted my map. If I fall in the hole, no one gets it."

That didn't seem to stop the banshee who chucked a chair at me. Two hobgoblins leapt on the banshee's back and that's when I understood that there seemed to be two opposing camps in the Rip Her Arm Off debate. One group wanted to find the entrance, while the other group wanted to prevent that from happening.

Sadly, both groups felt that killing me was the best the way to achieve their goals.

One of the banshees pulled an ancient tapestry from the wall and used it as a net to grapple one of the hobgoblins and push him down the hole.

"Do you know who gave me that?" Aki screamed with unbridled rage. "Athena. After I presided over her handling of the adoption proceedings of Erichthonius. That tapestry was one of a kind."

The tanuki twirled around, swinging his testicles like a shot-putter before releasing them in the direction of the banshee. The momentum of the toss sent the tanuki flying over the hole and clearing the twenty-foot chasm effortlessly. *Man oh man*, I thought. *If Thor swung what Aki had instead of a hammer, well, it would have been a totally different movie.*

Seeing him fly like that did give me an idea. I hoisted up the webbing that was still attached to my wrist and tied it around one of the branches of the chandelier. Then, loosening the webbing's grip around my wrist so that I could break free when needed, I ran up a branch away from the front door before leaping off.

Just as I hoped, my own momentum swung me back toward the door. I released the webbing at the last second and managed to swing over the heads of the brawling Others and toward the front door.

I'd like to tell you that being a "cat," I landed on my feet and tumbled past the fighting Others before running out that door. But the truth was, I landed on a garuda. Her soft, feathered body broke my fall (it was kind of like falling on a goose-feathered duvet) and I shimmied off her body like one trying to get off a half-inflated air mattress and ran outside.

Well, I tried to, but a large hand grabbed me, dragging me back. I turned to see one of the wendigos clawing at me. Wendigos have incredibly large mouths with razor-sharp teeth. All that beast needed to do was bite me at the elbow and he'd have the map.

From the way he pulled me up I realized that was exactly what he intended to do. I knew I had one chance to escape. I needed to time a kick to his groin at just the right moment to—

Before I could impress the world with my *Bend it Like Beckham* power and accuracy, the tail-end of a telescopic baton whacked the creature across the face, causing him to drop me.

I turned to see Jean reaching out a hand and saying in a terrible Austrian accent, "Come with me if you want to live."

↔

. . .

"Where the f—"

"Language," Jean interrupted as we ran to the tree line beyond the hotel's rock garden. "We might be running for our lives, but we're not running from our manners. And to answer the question you were going to ask … I was doing stuff. And you're welcome."

"Welcome?" I said between puffs. "I nearly got killed."

"Horse shoes and hand grenades," he said. "And speaking of hand grenades." He pulled out two grenades from his pocket, ripped out the pins with his teeth and dropped them as he ran.

I didn't look back, doubling my speed to get as far away from the explosive devices as possible. I also counted to three, bracing myself for the loud explosion that usually accompanied bombs.

But there was no boom, just a squeaking sound like air being let out of a balloon. So not a *boom* grenade. A smoke grenade?

I turned, expecting to see smoke coming out of the incendiary cylinders. Instead I saw nothing but several Others chasing after us. As soon as they got near the grenades, though, they stopped running as they yelped in obvious discomfort.

"Smell grenades," Jean said, pulling me behind the tree line. "Most Others have a heightened sense of smell, so the boys at the lab cooked those up. I'm told they're a wicked combination of skunk, rotting eggs and beached whale. I don't even want to know how you bottle beached whale."

We pushed on another thirty meters or so before Jean stopped.

"What are you doing?" I said. "They're right behind us."

He gave me a sardonic smile before lifting several fallen banana leaves, revealing a hole in the ground. He gestured for me to get in the hole. "Like I said, I was doing stuff."

Once inside, he covered us up and lifted a finger to his lips. "Shush."

We lay in silence in the cramped hole he'd dug, our bodies uncomfortably close to each other as we waited for the Others to run over us. We heard shouting and a few screeches and some yelling that slowly faded away as the Others ran deeper into the forest.

I realized that the smell grenades were designed to do more than just throw them off temporarily—they were to obscure our scent beneath these banana leaves.

When we were sure they'd all gone past, I pushed out of the hole. "You couldn't have made it bigger?"

"And what would have been the fun in that?" he said, pulling what looked like a cellphone from the 1980s out of his backpack. "Besides, don't flatter yourself. If I had spent more time making this hole any bigger, you'd be minus an arm right now." Jean tilted his head, considering this. "Which, if you think about it, would mean we'd manage with a smaller hole."

"Hilarious."

"Like I said, I'm funny in Paradise Lot."

"I'm sure you are," I said, turning away from him and assessing my next move. The hotel was locked away, filled with brawling Others, some of whom wanted access to the museum, others who wanted to stop that from happening.

Unless Aki and Harry turned out to be ninja, samurai or super-soldiers, it was unlikely we could return there and gain access to it that way. Even if we did, I didn't think we could find a safe way down that hole. As far as I could tell, the hole was so deep that the Others who'd fallen in were probably still falling.

I looked at my map, but it wasn't of any more help; the arrow still pointed at the hole.

"Neato," Jean said, grabbing my wrist with a bit too much familiarity for my liking. If he knew that he'd crossed a line, he made no indication of it as he stared intently at my arm.

Then he took his pinky finger and traced a blue line that seemed to run under the main map area where the red arrow pointed.

I pulled my arm away. "Hey—my body, my choice, perv."

"Oh get over yourself." He held out his hand, asking for my arm back. "Come on," he said, jerking his ring finger in with a "come hither" swagger.

I groaned and extended my arm out. Jean leaned in closer to examine the map and again he traced the blue line.

"Will you stop that?" I said.

He scratched his head, ignoring me. "What do you think this line is?"

Staring down at my arm, I followed the blue line as he traced it again. It zig-zagged, each zig or zag uneven in length, but all going in the same general direction as the red arrow. It reminded me of a complex weave where each layer was its own design and only when overlaying the individually crafted layers did you get the desired, intricate design.

The way it seemed to lay under the main map made me think that it was just decoration. After all, this was mystical in nature and it wasn't beyond the gods or Others or whatever celestial force had created this map to add a little decorative flair.

But as Jean continued tracing the line, I began to see a pattern to the blue lines. They weren't decoration like I had previously assumed. They were—

"Holy guacamole," I muttered, "this map is in 3D."

Jean snapped his finger before shaking his head. "That's exactly what I think," he said. "And what's more ..." He reached for his backpack and pulled out something that reminded me of a *Star Trek* tricorder (from the original series). Flipping it open, he showed me a green radar screen with three blips on it—two right next to each other, the third some distance away.

As the radar's arm passed around, it showed two lines that zig-zagged in an eerily similar pattern to the blue line on my arm.

"Here's the hotel, and these two blips are us. These lines are us running out of the hotel. As you can see, we ran pretty much in a straight line out of there." He traced the two green streaks that started at the hotel and ended at the blips—us. "And this third dot is Keiko. Here's her leaving the hotel, where she stops somewhere for ..."—he tapped the screen and some numbers appeared over the lines—"about twelve minutes. Then she descended into what I can only assume is a hole, before following a path that is almost identical to the blue line on your arm-map thingy."

I stared at the blips. There was no doubt that the blue lines followed the same pattern as Keiko's path. The other thing that was blatantly evident was that this asshole was stalking us. Without warning, I punched Jean square in the nose. Hard.

He went down, grabbing the bridge of his nose as two spurts of blood came out. "Ow," he cried. "What was that for?" But before I could answer, he raised a hand. "Never mind. I know what that was for … and you're not wrong for punching me. But you're not right, either. If I hadn't tracked you, I would have never known where Keiko went and, well …" —he pointed at his tricorder screen again—"and that she's stuck there."

"How do you know?"

"Because she hasn't moved in over an hour," he said, pointing at her dot with a blood-covered fingertip. "I doubt she's taking a nap."

I looked at the little number that hovered over Keiko's dot. Seventy-three minutes. Seventy-three minutes was a long time to be in one place, especially given that about forty minutes ago the world had rumbled as a new plane of existence competed for space in this one.

Keiko had gone off on her own, looking for … what? An entrance to the museum without us? A way to get to the prize first? I doubted that. From everything I knew about noro and everything I had seen in Keiko, she most likely wanted to stop Jean and his human military cohort from finding the entrance. And she didn't trust me enough to let me in on her plan.

Whatever her motives, they didn't matter. What mattered to me now was that Blue's granddaughter was in trouble.

"Let's go," I said, marching in the direction on his screen where Keiko had stopped to descend into the hole. The map was in 3D and it used different colors to represent depth. The deeper it went, the darker the colors.

"You're welcome," he called after me.

I turned. "No, you don't get to play the 'ends justify the means' card with me. Just because stalking us paid dividends doesn't make it right."

"Fair enough," he said. "But I'm surprised you're surprised. I mean, did you really think we'd offer you safe passage here without surveillance? We're military, ma'am. We're not really the trusting type."

"I know," I said. "And neither am I."

I tapped the screen two more times, revealing a fourth blip. I had noticed that he'd put the tracker on me back on the boat, just before the meres attack. When I went into the bowels of the boat and saw his pack, I'd paused for a second to take one of his unused trackers. When the hole opened up I'd thrown it in, figuring it would help us find a way down.

I showed him *my* planted blip.

He looked at it and then up at me in surprise before a comprehending smile dawned on his face. "Clever girl," he said with a chuckle. "Very clever indeed." And he bowed in my direction.

↔

We made our way to the spot where Keiko had clearly stopped for several minutes before she'd descended. But from where we stood there was no path down. As best as I could tell, we were standing in the heart of a tropical forest that was very much sans a hole.

And I would know: I was an expert tracker, having spent three hundred years honing my skills by tracking my human prey. If Keiko had been there, she'd left no indication of it.

There was simply no way for her to have been in that spot without crushing some brush, breaking some branches, leaving behind some sign of her—or human—presence.

To cover her tracks so thoroughly, she'd have to have burned time. And not just a little bit of it … lots of it.

Jean was thinking the same thing, because he was looking at his Mickey Mouse watch. He nodded before showing me the clock face. The second hand was spinning round manically, completing a full minute's rotation in less than a few seconds.

I scanned the trees, the ground, our surroundings, looking for the source of magic. Whatever burned time had hid itself as well, sacrificing time for ... for what?

The answer was obvious. For Keiko. She was a noro and just as she had summoned the makara—Meres Griffin (hey, I had to hand it to Jean, the name was catchy)—she had summoned something else to hide her tracks.

Something like—

I leapt to my right, throwing my body against the tree that stood not three feet away from me. Because I was looking around in a confused manner, I was able to hide that I had caught the glimmer of a kappa sitting so perfectly still in the shadows of the jungle that I might have mistaken the gray, turtle-like creature for a rock.

I grabbed the kappa and growled, "Stop it. Now!" as I applied pressure to the creature's neck, forcing it against the tree.

The kappa gulped but held fast. "Ahh," I heard Jean mutter from behind me, "He's not stopping anything. If anything, Mickey's working overtime now."

"Release your magic, foul beast," I snarled, "lest I show you the *final* meaning of mortality."

The creature's eyes did not waver and I could see that my threats weren't going to dissuade it from protecting Keiko. He was willing to sacrifice time for the noro. Lots of it.

But the mere fact that he wasn't attacking us also indicated that Keiko had instructed the kappa not to harm us. So whatever her plan was when she went off on her own, killing us wasn't part of it.

I felt Jean's hand on my shoulder. "Um, Kat ... I don't know when we went full *Game of Thrones*, and as much as I love watching you play bad cop, you mind giving me a shot?"

I let the kappa go and watched as Jean walked over to the creature and put a hand on its shoulder. I couldn't hear what Jean said, but I knew he was showing the creature his tricorder device. Jean talked and at one point the kappa even laughed.

Then Jean put a cross over his heart and the kappa creature nodded.

Stepping away from the kappa, he turned to me. "There? See, all you need is a little charm and to ask nicely. Point out the pros and cons of their actions and—"

I bent down, grabbed the largest rock I could find and threw it right at the back of the kappa's head as it tried to run away.

The creature fell unconscious. As soon as he was out his magic stopped flowing, revealing the crushed canopy brush and logs that had been hastily pulled over the hole so that anyone accidently stepping over the illusion wouldn't fall right through. But without the kappa's magic, even a child could see what could only be described as a human-sized gopher hole.

"You were saying?" I said with all the charm of a rattlesnake.

↔

We climbed down the hole until we reached a chasm that was easily high enough for Masamitsu the nuppeppo to stand and wide enough for three minotaurs to walk side by side. This tunnel wasn't naturally formed.

Someone—or rather, some*ones*—built it so that a small army could march through. The only questions were: who, and why?

As for the most important question—where did it lead?—that was answered by the ebbing tattoo on my arm. Even though the passage was quite dark (and I no longer had my vampiric see-in-the-dark eyesight ... sigh) I could clearly see the map's fluorescent lines. The gods really had thought of everything.

Including the multilayered map design, because as soon as we descended into the tunnel the map dropped down, erasing the previous overlay and showing the tunnel we were in. The red arrow pointed firmly in one direction down the hole—and toward Keiko.

"This way." Jean was holding a small flashlight in his teeth, looking at his tricorder.

"I know," I said, showing him my own mystical tracker, and started down the path.

As we walked I could feel Jean keeping pace a couple feet behind me, shining his lamp over my shoulder to illuminate the path ahead. How chivalrous of him.

He drew in a breath. I had spent enough time around humans to guess exactly what was coming: he wanted to defend why he was tracking us and put any negative feelings I had about him to rest.

"You know, I'm not such a bad guy," he started.

Nailed it.

"Nailed what?" he asked.

Talking out loud again—not that I cared. It had been pointed out that my nasty talking-out-loud habit seemed to coincide with the truth bursting out of me. And I didn't care if he heard my truth or not, especially when it came to him.

If he was curious as to what I'd nailed, he didn't pursue it further. "Actually," he said, "I am a bad guy. But I'm a bad guy doing the right thing. I'm trying to keep casualties to a minimum here and—"

"Casualties to a minimum," I snorted. "That's rich coming from the guy who took down two dragons with a harpoon gun."

"Hey, they knew exactly what they were getting into when they attacked the base. And yes, I did keep causalities to a minimum by stopping those dragons from taking more human lives. Also, if you recall, I kept the suffering to a minimum by stopping my jerk comrades-in-arms from torturing the poor beast."

I thought back to how he had stopped the other humans from tormenting the dragon and how, in as merciful a way as possible, he had ended the creature's life. It had been a point for him. A big one.

But I shook my head. "Just because you showed a moment of compassion doesn't make you a good guy. Or—how did you put it?— 'a bad guy doing the right thing.'"

"How do you figure?" he said, the light temporarily shooting to the tunnel's ceiling as he lifted his hands up in exasperation.

As soon as the light was back on the path, I answered him. "Because you're trying to claim the museum and all its contents for the human army."

"Actually, I'm trying to stop a bunch of badass magical items from getting into the hands of Others who know exactly how to use them. And that is … how did you put it?"—he paused before he echoed my own words—"rich coming from the girl who's 'after her soul, no matter the cost.' "

"Excuse me?"

"You heard me. You've got a map to this place on your arm. A map, by the way, that you never told me how you obtained. For all I know you killed a litter of cynocephalus puppies to get it."

Before I could think of some witty answer about the origins of the map that involved the words, "None of your business," he continued, "If you were such a good girl, then you wouldn't be here with it on your arm for any creature with fangs to rip it off you."

"First of all, I had no idea this museum was such a damn popular place. I thought I was going to do a little private tomb raiding and be done with it. Secondly, you guys are the ones who forced me to come here."

He nodded. "That we did. With almost no resistance from you."

"Resistance?" I twirled around to face this jerk, still walking backward just in case my abrupt stop would cause any unwanted bumping into each other. "You're the guys who are holding my friends captive and—"

And just as I was about to hit him with a retort worthy of the Retorting Hall of Fame, I took another step back and my foot slipped on something unnaturally smooth given that we were in an underground cavern.

I fell forward as my body slid back. I reached out for Jean, but it was too late—I was already sliding down a path that was growing increasingly steep.

As I rushed down toward whatever was waiting for me below, I heard Jean yell after me, "You were saying?"

Jerk.

↔

I slid down the pathway on what felt like marble until I fell into a black, cavernous pit with a painful thump. I couldn't see anything, but I could smell it. This place smelled like … like … the Catacombs of Paris.

Not an entirely unpleasant smell, but an unusual one. The Catacombs of Paris were a series of underground crypts with thousands of human skeletons decorating the walls. The old bones, stripped of flesh and the meat of muscles and veins and sinew, had a distinct smell to them, something akin to a dusty old attic and that new car smell.

Like I said, not unpleasant, but distinct.

There was also a hint of fresh, non-human blood (after years of drinking human blood, I could not only distinguish human blood from Other blood, but I could also tell you a lot about a person from how their blood smelled. In the vampire communities I was somewhat famous for having a particularly refined nose).

I stood, but I was terrified that I'd fall down another slide or fall deeper into an already deep hole, so I didn't move. I looked at my map tattoo, the red, neon glow of an arrow that pointed straight ahead no matter what direction I faced. There were no more blue and orange cavern lines, which meant that I had fallen into a hole within a hole. Unfortunately, the neon glow wasn't strong enough to illuminate my surroundings at all.

Great.

I looked straight up. In the far, far distance, I saw the glow of a hole. The hotel's entrance, but it was so far up that the light from the hotel itself didn't reach down here to illuminate the ground.

This place was pitch black, but not silent.

I could hear breathing not far from where I stood.

"Keiko," I said, "are you hurt?"

There was an almost imperceptible sigh as Keiko's voice said, "No, I am fine. *Demo watashi wa baka desu.* Stepping so carelessly and falling here."

"I wouldn't beat yourself up about falling. I was careless and fell, too. But even if I had been careful, with the way that incline suddenly appeared, I'm pretty sure that was a trap set up by a god (who probably had a minotaur consultant or something)."

Keiko didn't answer, apparently not taking solace in me falling, too. I guess misery doesn't always love company. "Fine," I said. "Bruised ego aside, are you hurt?"

"Bruised pride and hip, but yes, I am well."

"Good. Then perhaps you can tell me what in the blue flames of Tartas you're doing here?"

Another sigh before Keiko growled, "My grandmother told me that you are an honorable person. But what I see is one who only cares for herself."

"Not you, too," I said. "Let me guess, how could I work with the Americans and lead them to this place? Right?"

Silence.

"Right?" I said with more emphasis.

"Hai," she said.

"Well, what if I told you that I was using them to find this place? That my plan is to get my soul and then shut down the whole operation?"

"Plan?" she said. "Please explain."

"Sure," I said, "I'll tell you my genius plan if you tell me yours. You know, let's have a little quid pro quo or tit for tat or whatever."

Silence, followed by another *"Hai."*

"Jean planted trackers on us. That's in part how we knew you were trapped."

"Mukatsuko."

"Exactly. Still, it was predictable, and during the meres attack I stole a couple of his trackers to put him off our scent. As soon as I got my chance, I was going to attach them to a monkey or a mokumokuren or whatever I found and send him on a wild goose chase while we—and note I am saying *we*—found the place. Pretty straightforward plan."

"And if he followed us?"

"Knock him out, tie him up. That kind of stuff. Look, I'll be the first to admit that I hadn't calculated everything." I looked up at the hole. "In fact, I miscalculated a shit-ton of stuff. There was a lot I didn't know about the museum, like that it exists on a completely different plane, so I'm improvising here. But I can promise you this: no matter what happens, I will do everything in my power to make sure the military doesn't get their hands on the place. Both the human and Other ones," I added.

Keiko was silent and because I couldn't see her, I had no idea how she was reacting to my little confession. Whatever her reaction was, she was weighing my words against whether or not she believed them enough to trust me with her secret.

"We noro knew of this place for centuries," she said.

Evidently she had decided to trust me.

"When the god Izanagi-no-Mikoto locked Izanami-no-Mikoto away here because death had already ravaged her body, he entrusted us with a lock of sorts. He made us promise that we would never let anyone but the gods enter this place. I am here to fulfill that promise."

I paused, taking this all in, marveling at how everyone and their mother had an interest in the museum. The human and Other armies were trying to find it. The noro were trying to stop that from happening.

Then there was the matter of the nio and shisa guardians, and given that they had also tried to kill Keiko, I figured the noro weren't responsible for them. Then there was the yokai, who seemed determined to help me get here.

"So if you're so hell-bent on stopping me, why did you help us with the meres? Or guide us to the hotel?"

"I owe you a debt for what you did for my grandmother. Also ..." her voice trailed off.

"Also?"

"You had the map and I needed it to find this place."

So that was it. She was another person in the long list of peeps who wanted to use me for my arm. I was starting to feeling like Google Maps.

"So you found it without me. How?"

More silence.

"Come on, Keiko. We're probably going to die in this cavern. No point in holding back on me now."

"I could—I could always see the map."

"What? How?"

"Not me, but the mokumokuren."

"So you're behind the yokai?"

"No," she said. "The ghosts are being summoned by something else. But the mokumokuren, they are friends of the noro and they can see all."

"And let me guess: those little bastards figured out that the map was in 3D and that the blue and orange lines weren't decorative, but deeper pathways in. And as soon as we were close enough, the map updated itself, showing you enough about how to find this place that you came here on your own."

"*Hai.*"

"Sneaky."

"Necessary. I must close this place once and for all."

"With the lock from Izanami-no-Mikoto?"

"*Hai.*"

"Great plan. Too bad we're stuck here."

"Perhaps I can help with that, ladies?" a voice said as a light shined on us.

Jean.

↔

. . .

"So, I guess I'll add eavesdropping to your laundry list of virtues," I said. "How much did you hear?"

"I don't know. I showed up just at the point where you were talking about monkeys and wild goose chases," he sneered, turning the light on himself so we could see his face.

Then he tossed the light to me, the flashlight landing a foot in front of me. I picked it up and what I saw was a graveyard of the dead. Others, but also humans littered the ground, and not just from earlier today. Their blood was fresh, but there were plenty of bones from creatures who had fallen into this hole years ago. Centuries ago. There was so much death here that I wouldn't have been surprised if the fine dust covering the ground was just the ancient remains of those who died long, long ago.

I wasn't allowed to wallow in my shock at the macabre for long before Jean said, "I also heard about her lock and I think it's a pretty good deal. I'd like to help."

"Help with what?" I asked.

"Help lock this place down."

"*Usuki*," Keiko spat.

"I concur—liar. You just want us to lead you to the place and—"

"Ah, ah, ah," he said, pulling out a second flashlight and turning it on. He threw it to Keiko. "Believe it or not, I also think this place falling into human hands is a catastrophic mistake. Don't get me wrong: given the choice between human and Other hands, I pick human. But given the choice between human and no hands ..." He turned on a third flashlight and pulled out something from his back-pack. He lit what was in his hands so that we could read the *C4* printed on the front of the pack with an explosives symbol under it. "I pick no hands," he said.

↔

195

. . .

"How can we trust you?" Keiko asked.

"I don't suppose Scout's Honor would work with you?"

Keiko gave Jean a curious look. "He's trying to be funny," I said, clarifying what Jean meant to a Japanese noro priestess who clearly hadn't heard of the Boy Scouts of America before.

"He should try harder," Keiko answered.

Jean groaned. "Look, I get that you don't trust me. The truth is, I wouldn't trust me either if I was in your shoes, but I don't want any more fighting than necessary."

"How about no fighting at all?" Keiko said.

"That would be nice," Jean said with all the sincerity of an adult appraising a toddler's drawing. "But impractical. There will be blood. There will be a war between humans and Others. That's coming and nothing's going to stop that. Especially not the return of some third-rate, axis of evil gods raising the dead to complicate things. We can work to minimize the losses … on both sides," he said, raising his voice so that the last two words echoed. "Or we can't. I've already told you where I stand on the issue."

"Yes, but—"

"Look Keiko, I get you want a guarantee, so here it is: either I'm on your side and there's nothing to worry about, or I'm some evil dick-head who's going to betray you the first chance I get. I promise I'm the former, but if I turn out to be the latter, then you two can gang up on me and take me out. Shouldn't be hard for an ex-vamp and samurai ninja, right?"

Keiko snorted at this.

"He's right, Keiko," I said. "This is the best deal we're going to get."

"No," she said. "How can I trust you when your motivations are so selfish?"

I didn't know wanting my soul back was selfish, I thought.

"It is when the fate of life as we now understand it hangs in the balance," she said.

GoneGodDamn—I really had to stop thinking out loud. "Fine," I said, "it's selfish. But you don't know what it's like not having it be a part of me. It's like—"

"Do you forsake your quest for your soul for the greater good?"

"Excuse me?"

"Do you forsake your quest for your soul for the greater good?" she repeated. The noro priestess stared at me with burning eyes, waiting for my answer.

"I … I don't know," I said. I knew I could lie to her and say that I'd give up my quest for the greater good, but as desperate as she was for an answer, so was I. After all, I had spent the last few months trying to atone for all the evil shit I did as a vampire, and here I had an opportunity to actually do something that would save hundreds of lives.

Thousands, even. More lives than I'd taken in my three hundred years of neck biting.

This would be proof that I was finally a good person. And if not a good person, then at least a person capable of doing good. All I had to do was close the museum forever, lock away my soul and walk away.

But inside there was my soul, the very thing that imbued my being with the desire to do good. It was also a part of me that I doubted I could live without. The emptiness, the depression—I knew myself: it would get to me. Maybe not right away, but eventually I would succumb and end myself.

Lock away my soul, die a slow and mentally torturous death.

And in doing so, save thousands.

Given all that I'd done, that sounded like a fair exchange to me.

I stepped over to Keiko. I could see her concern illuminated in the lamplight. "Keiko," I said, "I don't know if I can forsake my quest for my soul. If I see a chance to get it back, I'm going to go for it."

Keiko started to protest, but I lifted a hand before she could get a word out. "All I do know is that I will chose them—humans and Others—over myself."

Keiko stared at me for a long, uncomfortable moment, unsure whether to accept my answer or not.

She might have kept staring at me had Jean not interrupted our awkward soul (well, soul-less in my case) gaze. "That's the best deal you're going to get," he said.

With the spell broken, I gestured for Jean to help us out. "Good, I'm glad that's settled. Now I don't know about you, but I'm tired of sitting around in this hole."

↔

Jean threw us down a rope that I used to shimmy up the supernaturally created hole.

Whereas before I had thought that the slick incline was a trap set up by the gods, now that my feet were sliding against the same slippery material on the side of this hole, I realized it wasn't a trap at all.

Well, a trap set by *the gods*, that is. The lining was marble, but not the kind made through stone masonry. This was naturally forming, caused by unexpected, extreme heat that cooled just as suddenly as it heated up.

I guess that's what happens when an alternate dimension tries to overlay itself onto another plane of existence without the gods or magic to help it along. The laws of nature take over, and when nature wants to get something done, it usually does it hot and furious.

Keiko and I got to the incline that we had originally slid down and I saw that Jean was using hiking spikes to keep his balance. He handed us two climbing axes. "There's a hole a few feet up from here. It leads … well, I have no idea where it leads, but I figure anywhere is better than here."

Using some kind of high-tech spike gun that was basically a super-sized nail gun—think the Super Soaker version of a water pistol—he led us to a hole wide enough for us to crawl through. Unlike the rest of the veins, this particular hole wasn't made of the same smooth, marble-like rock.

Once we were safely perched, I looked at my tattoo. It pointed down the hole, indicating a sharp left turn at the end. This led us to other pathways that branched into yet more pathways. All the while, my tattoo guided us through a maze worthy of Daedalus's Labyrinth. But unlike Theseus, we didn't have a ball of thread to guide us—we had a celestial GPS.

And I could see why everyone wanted my map; no one would be able to find this place without it.

After hours of crawling, we made our way down to a path that—according to my arm—ended in a clearing or cavern or whatever you called a big open space underground. A red dot hovered at the far end of the space.

"If I'm reading my tattoo correctly, we aren't too far off from our destination," I said. "But before we get to wherever *there* is, what do we know and what's the plan?"

Jean touched his backpack. "I can plant these so no one will be able to knock on that front door again."

Keiko shook her head. "Not good enough. You will only slow the Others or humans down—you will not stop them." She pulled out something that looked like a piece of thin thread rolled into a ball. "Use this."

"This?" I said, taking it from her. "I could snap this with a … a …" I pulled at the string, but it was tight as iron. I had encountered this unbreakable iron with Jack the Giant; he wore an impossibly heavy pendant that was held by one of these chains around his neck for penance. "Humph," I said. "A gleipnir chain?"

Keiko nodded. "But not just any gleipnir chain. This was the very thread used to leash Fenrir. Once a knot is tied, it cannot be broken."

"I don't know—my knots are pretty lousy. I was never a Girl Scout."

"I was," Jean said with a wee bit too much enthusiasm. His cheeks turned bright red before he muttered, "I mean, Boy Scout. I was a Boy Scout."

Keiko glided past his faux pas way too fast for me, getting right back to business. "Place that thread at the entrance of the museum to lock its doors. No one and nothing will be able to break that bond until the rotation is complete and this domain leaves our world. Even then, I suspect we will be locking that door forever."

With my soul inside, I thought (uncharacteristically, in my head).

"OK, so here we go," I said, crawling the last few feet into the large, cavernous room.

The tunnel let us out onto a path that wound down to a landing where a long rope bridge hung over another impossibly deep cavern. At the far end of the rope bridge was a door with three kanji: *Sun, Heaven* and *Fields*. The same three kanji I'd seen on Harry's necklace.

The entrance to the museum.

That was the good news. The bad news was that, guarding the other side of the rope bridge was what looked like a man in a samurai demon mask. And although he looked fairly normal (mask aside) he wore a plethora of weapons on his body.

"*Kuso,*" Keiko said. "*Benkei desu.*"

↔

Staring at the seriously scary dude guarding the bridge, I muttered, "Of course there has to be a samurai warrior. I mean, we're in Japan. My trip wouldn't be complete unless I fought a samurai, right?"

And not just an ordinary samurai, either, I thought. He was something else. For one thing, he wore a pair of wooden shoes with two horizontal stilts under each sole, giving the already tall figure an extra four inches. Talk about uncomfortable. I'd worn stilettos that were practically comfy slippers by comparison.

Poor fashion choices aside, this guy had a whole bunch of terrifying weapons on his back. From the rock ledge on which we stood, I couldn't see them all, but I did catch a glimpse of a naginata, a nokogiri, a kumade, and a masakari.

"Not a samurai," Keiko said. "Warrior monk."

"How can you tell? He's wearing one of those masks," Jean said.

"Urasai," Keiko growled at us in Japanese. *"Honto ni, atadatchi ga mukatsuku."*

Jean looked at Keiko uncomprehendingly.

"Keiko thinks you're annoying. Really, really annoying." I didn't add that she thought we were *both* annoying.

"I do have that effect on women," Jean said, not missing a beat. "So, do you think he's alive?"

Looking down at the warrior monk, I knew exactly why he was asking. The figure didn't move. At all. I would have thought him a statue if his robes weren't loosely draped over his chest, revealing finely toned flesh. But given that his chest didn't rise and fall with breath, I considered whether he might be some weird Japanese taxidermy project.

"Benkei. He is the warrior monk who once served Minamoto no Yoshitsune. It was legend that when he died, the gods took his soul so that he could continue his guardianship. I guess this is where his service continues. It is also legend that in his lifetime only Minamoto no Yoshitsune was able to defeat him in battle."

"Yay," I said, taking out my telescopic baton.

↔

I had barely managed to get to the landing when Benkei animated, raising his naginata to meet my baton. I expected him to charge me, but he didn't, standing right at the bridge's edge.

What he did do was let out a thunderous growl that ended in flat, monotone "um." How very zen of him.

I thought it was his warrior's roar. By the GoneGods I wished it was, but he wasn't centering himself as he prepared for battle.

He was calling for help.

Help that made itself known when dozens of nio and shisa started pouring out of the walls and pathways.

Apparently the Heralds weren't the only ones who could summon supernatural body guards.

Double yay.

↔

"Of course there's a samurai," I said as the beast of a man swung his giant naginata at me. This was going to be one hell of a fight … and I knew the longer the battle raged on, the more chances I had of being split in two.

That's why I focused on getting behind Benkei and onto the rope bridge. Evading his naginata and nokogiri, I managed to end up exactly where he didn't want me to be.

Between him and the museum.

I was making my way down the rope when I heard Keiko call out, "Watch out for his hizuchi." As if I hadn't see the six-inch flat bit of the hammer slamming toward me. A hizuchi—so much for no fancy Japanese name for a warhammer.

I figured he was going to chase after me and nail me through the wooden bridge's planks and down to the cave floor hundreds of feet below. Well, screw that. If anyone was going to end me Wile E. Coyote style, they'd have to do it to my face.

I stopped running and turned to face him, placing a hand on the rope railing of the bridge. He was heavy and the second he started on the bridge, the thing would shake. A lot. Possibly enough to knock me off and save him the trouble of knocking me off.

Maybe he was counting on that, too. Much more efficient than sledgehammering me.

But the monk didn't charge toward me. Instead he removed his demon mask, revealing a pleasant, youthful face. He narrowed his eyes and pursed his lips as if conflicted.

What could he possibly be conflicted about? I thought. He wanted to stop me from getting to the other side and the only way to do so would be to engage me here on the bridge. Right?

I barely had time to consider what else was running through the ancient warrior's mind when he swung his hizuchi like a golf club, knocking out the pegs that secured the ropes to his side of the bridge.

He'd figured out an even more efficient method of killing me.

The bridge dipped away and just like that, I was airborne. I didn't have a chance.

As I fell, I wondered what dying without a soul does to a person.

↔

Here I was again, weightless and about to die. What a way to ring in the new year.

And once again, the thought came to me: *Maybe that wouldn't be such a bad thing.*

I'd spent so long *not* feeling, and the quest to retrieve my soul seemed so impossible in that moment, that I wondered why I didn't choose the easier route. The simpler route.

It was like being a vampire again, choosing what felt right *in that moment.* That was how I'd spent three hundred years until—

Blue.

Until a little girl reminded me of who I'd been. That no matter what, I still had humanity.

Even if I didn't have a soul.

I wasn't ready to die. I wanted to live—needed to live. I reached out for the bridge's old, wooden boards, my hand ripping through three of them before I finally latched onto a plank that didn't crumble under my weight.

Climbing the rope bridge like a ladder, I made it up to the platform. I turned to see Keiko and Jean fighting side by side to fend off the nio and shisa. They were about to be overrun and there was no way for me to get back to them.

What was worse: Benkei had turned to help finish a job that his nio and shisa were having no trouble finishing. I pulled out the gleipnir thread, ready to lock the museum away. My friends were going to die, and the least I could do was finish the mission.

As my hand reached out to the two large metal rings that served as door handles, I pulled. I had meant to thread the loops, but I pulled. I didn't know why. Was I compelled by some force to look inside, or perhaps the curiosity of looking inside a place created by the gods was too much?

Or maybe I was just selfish and wanted to see if opening the door was enough to summon my soul back into me.

I hated myself, but the truth was it was me being selfish. Definitely that.

I pulled and as soon as the door opened, the nio and shisa stopped fighting. So too did Benkei. It was like the museum's door was some kind of switch that turned them all off.

The nio and shisa froze mid-attack. One minute they were moving and the next they weren't. Only Benkei moved, turning to face me and watch as I walked inside.

Entering, the last thing I heard was Keiko shout, "No, you must lock the—" before the museum door closed under its own power.

And inside was unlike any museum I'd ever seen before.

↔

The first indication that this wasn't your typical museum: there were long, winding corridors that wove around in every direction, and the walls were lined with magic items. Yes, impossible items of massive power.

But the walls were also littered with the bodies of mummified creatures that lined them. And by mummified, I don't mean embalmed creatures wrapped in bandages. I mean they were frozen like Han Solo.

But unlike Han Solo's carbonite tomb, these guys were in full color, as if some Warhammer geek had painted them to look exactly like they did when they were alive. That, or whatever magic had frozen them also kept their brilliant coloring.

I recognized a few of the creatures: Typhon with his hundred dragon heads, the furies with their coal-black bodies, the dragon Hydra, the Erlking—the original games hunter who liked to trap worthy opponents and hunt them down (I'm pretty sure the Predator was modeled after this guy).

The only guys this place was missing were the Devil, Sauron and Cthulhu.

But those were the creatures I recognized. There were plenty of bashees and skin walkers and wendigos and goblins and even a few angels frozen here. They were probably the evil that never made it into the history books.

This wasn't a museum. This was the place the gods disposed of their more troublesome creations. And my soul was trapped somewhere in here.

Shaking off the evilness of this place, I looked at my map. It had narrowed, only displaying one corridor now with a red dot near my wrist. Walking along this hall that held items of unimaginable power displayed on both walls, I saw that the corridor ended with a single, unassuming door at the end. From the position of the dot, I knew that my soul resided just beyond that door. All I needed to do was open it and walk through.

I took several steps forward, my heart thumping with the anticipation of finally getting my soul back.

But the excitement slowly dissipated as I approached the door, turning into doubt and fear. The thought that I was doing something horribly wrong swam through my head as a flood of memories overwhelmed me.

I thought about the mermaid fight, fighting with the nio and shisa. All that destruction because of me. Sure, these guys would be heralding away, but their hopes would be fulfilled in the same way all fanatics are when waiting for a comet or an eclipse or whatever other naturally occurring event that they give meaning to results in … nothing.

Except these guys weren't going to get nothing if they got a hold of my arm. They were going to awake a god—or gods—who had been killed for a reason. They were the worst of the worst, and I possessed the only road map to their hiding place.

If they were resurrected, then it would be all-out war.

If this celestial turning were to come and go without some asshole god coming to life … well, there'd still be a fight coming. Nothing would stop that, but there would be no rallying point for the Others to gather around and the will to fight would fizzle.

Thousands of lives would be saved.

That wasn't all. Gods or no gods, I held the map to a magical stockpile of weapons that would be used for evil. Again, I *was* the map.

And all because I wanted my soul back. I wanted to feel something other than this emptiness inside me. I wanted to be human again.

You can end this all now, I thought. *Just step to the right or left and pull off any one of the weapons hanging on these walls. One step to the left and cut your throat with the spearhead that stabbed Jesus. One step to the right and turn the sword that Goliath used when facing David on yourself.*

It's hard to explain what goes through your mind when you're considering ending it all. Not much. Everything. All I know is that at that moment, I saw a world being ripped in two because of me.

This could all end with one step. One step and the world would be a better place. One step and my pain would be over.

One easy step.

"Well, fuck easy," I growled. "I deserve a second chance, just like you."

Shaking off the overwhelming feeling of despair, I pulled at the unassuming door and walked into a room that wasn't there. I mean, it was because I was in it, but there were no walls, no ceiling and no floor to speak of. It was like I was walking into the void, with the only object that offered perspective being the door I had entered through hovering in the blackness behind me.

What else was missing? Any shelves that could have possibly held a jar with my friggin' soul in it.

What the f—? I started to think, fully aware it was in my out loud voice, when I heard an ominous boom. "Welcome, Katrina Darling. We have waited so long to meet you."

"Meet me?" I repeated, my head woozy as the words spoken not only seemed to come from both outside and *inside* my head, but also lingered like a song you can't stop humming.

"Yes, my dear," spoke another, softer—distinctly female—voice. It also carried the hint of a Japanese accent. The voice purred, "So nice to finally meet you."

"Meet you ... again," spoke a third voice. This one sounded like my father's voice. No, my mother's. Egya's? Deirdre's? Justin's? All those people's voices and a hundred more came to mind as I tried to place this one, and that's when it hit me that this third voice sounded like everyone I'd ever known all speaking to me at once.

"For on this day ..." thundered the first voice.

"We will rise ..." purred the second voice.

"And it is all because of you ..." chorused the legion of voices.

I gulped and in my own meek and unsure voice, croaked, "Me?"

27

AN ENDING OF SORTS

I waited for the dawn to come with Blue in my arms, and as the first ray of sunlight peaked over the horizon, I placed her body a few feet in front of me.

I was about to catch fire and I wasn't sure how much she could feel in her comatose state. The last thing I wanted to do was cause her more pain.

I had failed this little girl, this Blue, the only being I had loved since I had turned into the monster I was today.

Maybe it was the exhaustion or the thought that I would live on when she would not. Maybe it was because Blue reminded me of what it meant to be human again and those memories carried with them a horrible guilt for all the lives I had taken as a monster, a vampire.

Maybe it was because Blue was a witch and had cast a spell on me, forcing me to do the right thing by finally killing the monster I had become.

Or maybe it was simply the absolute and complete grief I felt at losing her.

Whatever it was, I welcomed the peace that would come with finally ending at dawn.

I closed my eyes and waited for the light of the morning to wash over me, but instead of feeling its warm light followed by the destruction of fire, my body was shaded.

Opening my eyes, I saw a two-meter-high wall towering over me, blocking the sun's rays from touching my flesh.

"Nani sugu?" the wall asked. "What are you doing?"

ALSO BY RAMY VANCE

Mortality Bites Series

Mortality Bites

Family Matters

Superhero Me!

Orphaned Follies

Dawn of a Thousand Sunsets

Three Dead Gods

Run, Kat, Run

Encantado Dreams

The Heaviest of Burdens

Looking for a great deal? Grab these book bundles...

Setting Fires with Dragons - complete series

Mortality Bound - complete series

GoneGod World - Complete series

Series Starter - Bundle